The Boy That Wanted to Fly

By:
James E. Harris III

PRESS

Xulon Press
2301 Lucien Way #415
Maitland, FL 32751
407.339.4217
www.xulonpress.com

Printed in the United States of America.

ISBN-13: 9781498480840

Chapter 1

Wishful Thinking

We all have had dreams of doing remarkable things. Some dream of making a better life for themselves and their loved ones, others dream of becoming successful and powerful. These are the things that man sees as attainable, but what about the unattainable, what about the dreams of running on water, or self-healing? The world calls such people fools for daring to dream of such things. I guess I'm one of them. Hello, my name is Jason Jr. and I often dream of flying and one day I believe I will. No, I am not talking about with a flying machine that I will invent, or become a pilot, I'm talking about me, literally flying! I don't know why I think or dream such a thing is possible, but I do believe we humans are capable of doing anything that we set our minds to. I may be young, but I know our minds border on the supernatural call it instinct, but I believe I was put here on this earth to show this fact to be true.

Like I said, my name is Jason Abrams, Jr. and I am fifteen years old and in two months, I will be sixteen, the age when teens can drive. Honestly, that isn't my goal—flying is—and because of this my family and friends call me JJ the dreamer. I have done just about everything to try to fly, ranging from Parkour training to try to get more air all the way to gymnastics for strengthening my body and becoming agiler. I have even had to throw a few boxing and karate classes in the mix for the bullies who would push me around for wearing a leotard, but hey, I had to learn how to use my body's momentum to get up into high places. I have broken more bones than I can count and once my dream of flying almost ended permanently.

I was about twelve years old when I went on my first parkour run with some buddies of mine. Parkour is a physical discipline of training to move freely over and through any terrain using only the abilities of the body through running, jumping, climbing, and quadrupedal movement. I was scouting around for people who knew the art and knew it well. I had no time to waste with beginners; I had a dream to reach and I wanted to take the fast road. Idiot! Well, I ran into these three guys named Roy, Mark, and John and man, were they the best at what they did! I just happened to be walking down an alley in Newsbury, Ohio and I looked up, daydreaming about, you guessed it, flying. All of a sudden, I saw them jumping across rooftops and down fire escapes like they were nothing. If I needed any proof that a man could hold his own in the air with the birds, they were it! I ran my hardest, trying to follow them everywhere they went, when all of a sudden, I was spotted by Roy, the leader of the group. He laughed at me for trying to keep up with them and even egged everyone else to run faster so they could lose me. But they couldn't lose me. I had my ticket to get in the air and I wasn't about to lose it around a couple tight corners or red lights. I had to catch them and catch them I did.

Roy looked at me after jumping down from a steep ledge and said, "Hey small fry why you followin' us so hard?"

I simply replied, "Because I want to fly and you guys are my ticket to doing it."

He just stared at me like I was crazy because he probably thought I was. His bewildered gaze turned into a smirk as he said, "Meet us at fifty-fifth and Lockhart tomorrow at seven o'clock and don't be late."

The night couldn't have gone by fast enough and the following morning I rushed out of the house telling my mother I was going out for my daily run. I left out the specifics because I didn't want her to worry. After all, I had been talking about flying since I was five years old and now that I was twelve and still harping about it, she had started to get more concerned about me. I went to the location at the time specified, but I didn't see them. There were a few abandoned buildings around, one having a fire escape on it, so I decided to climb it to get a better view of things. No sooner had I gotten to the roof did I feel the rushing wind of Roy, Mark, and John running past me and jumping to the lower building that was right next to us. All I could hear was Mark saying, "Keep up little pilot!"

It hit me they had tested me. They had passed my expectations but I had to pass theirs in order for them to take me on. Mind you, this is my first parkour run, so I had no clue of how they were able to jump down a few stories, roll, and get up running without a scratch, but I had no time to let ignorance stop me. I did what I knew how to do. I found some stairs and jumped as many as I could. There was an old rickety boardwalk leading to the building where they were, so I ran across it almost falling through because of a hole in the bridge. I found that when I got to the roof, they were already three buildings away. I could see John running and pointing back laughing at me saying, "He can't even keep up!"

I felt like a failure, and I couldn't let this opportunity of flight slip through my fingers. I had to keep up, so I started moving my legs faster and jumping over the obstacles and before I knew it, I was at the edge of the second building. I saw a fire escape that could take me to the roof of the third. The only way to get to it and keep up with the already out of sight parkour runners was to jump.

My heart beat in the back of my throat and I couldn't decide what to do. Should I go home and give up on this dream of flight or do I swallow my fear and make this leap that could help me attain the unattainable? Truth be told, I leaned toward that first choice because of the insanity of this plan. I mean, men aren't meant to fly. How could I have let such a childish wish get me to this point? I was at the top of a three-story building, trying to keep up with people who have probably done this for years before going out on what looked to be a child's run to them. I turned around and got off the ledge so I could find a way down, but I was stopped when I saw a dove. We locked eyes for a moment and it was odd how we stared at each other for what felt like hours. The eyes of the dove are black as night and the longer I stared at them, the more lost I was, and the more peace I felt. It's like I was meant to be here on this roof, chasing these runners and this dove was my witness to see if I wanted the reality of flight within my body, to have the wind

5

blowing on my face, moving hundreds of miles per hour across sea and land, to places that would be otherwise out of reach for me. I asked myself the most important question: "Do you want it?"

The trance ended and the dove took flight beyond the building and I found myself taking the latter of the options. I jumped for the fire escape and almost had it, but almost didn't make it. I fell several stories into a dumpster and knocked unconscious. I heard faint sounds of sirens and people talking as I was rushed to the hospital. All I can was, *My momma's gonna kill me.* It was weird, but I was in peace amongst the pain I felt in my body. Maybe it was the morphine, but I knew I accomplished something by jumping to that escape. I knew I had faced the possible fear of heights and falling, after all, one trying to fly can't be afraid of the sky, can he?

I drifted in and out, but I heard my mother and father weeping along with my kid brother and sister. All I could think was, *I can't be this selfish again to put them through this type of pain,* wondering if I am going to live or die all because I didn't want to wait and take time to do it right. Next time, I would do it the right way and get the training before going off half-cocked. If this dream is worth having, then it is worth the time it takes to make it happen, which is what my dad always said.

I wanted to live to experience flight and I want to do it while my family was still living. I could not give them a heart attack again. Time passed and I was still in and out. I felt the love of my mother's kisses on my forehead one day and my father's embrace the next. I heard my brother encourage me by saying, "Who is gonna dream if you're not around?" And my sister said, "I'm gonna tell dad if you don't get up!"

Man, even when I'm down, she's still such a snitch. I heard the doctor talk to my father and mother in front of me, saying I may never walk again because the fall damaged my vertebrae severely and if I did get out of that bed, I would be confined to a wheelchair. Trust me, it wasn't long before that registered in my mind and I knew it was time for recovery. *How can I fly if I can't get up from this bed?* I had to get up, but in the days that followed, I found myself more conscious of the fact that I couldn't move. Man, if you could measure the energy I put into trying to move my whole body, you'd be able to use it to power a city. Was this it? Was this where I was going to be confined for the rest of my life just because I believed I could fly? *No!* I could not think like that again. It was the rooftop all over again. I would not let this bed or anything else stop me from reaching my goal! Not ignorance of the art of flying that the birds covet, not anxiety that caused me to fail, not people who said I couldn't. I believed I could and I started by moving out of this bed. And in the midst of my rage and tension late in the middle of the night, I felt my toe move. It actually moved and I felt tension in my body! I know it was not much, but by that time I had spent a week or two in that bed and besides that pain, I could feel nothing. *I'm doing it, I'm making progress.*

A week had gone by since I felt my toe move and I was able to move my legs and arms but just a little bit. *Good, because I need those.* The nurses were amazed at my recovery and the doctors had no answer for my mother. All she did when she came to the hospital was cry over me and begged me not to do parkour again. I said a small "yes" but I did intend to run again, but with training. My father was happy, but it was odd he didn't seem shocked. My brother had just busted his head during football practice and he was scared stiff. My little sister fell down one step and he treated her like she was injured in the Vietnam War, but with me, he seemed a little calmer. Maybe he was just being strong for my mother—after all, I'd hate to have both of them crying over me. *Please, let's not go down that road.*

Another week passed and they had just taken off the bandages that were on my feet and changed them to more loose bandages so I could move my toes more. What was odd about this day was my dad was the only one who visited, but he brought some strange woman with him. He lucky he's alone or momma would have had his head because she was not at all ugly. Like a ten. She looked like a nurse and she examined me to see how I was doing. It was nothing unusual; I had been checked on since I got there, but the way she looked at me is like there is something special about me or even strange.

She said, "Hello JJ, I am nurse May and I was checking to see if you were okay."

I answered with a yes and looked at her like, "Seriously? I have been here a while and I am recovering like nobody's business and you are asking me if I am okay?"

She went on to say, " Do you feel strange?"

I answered, "No," but in my head, I said, "you must be the pretty slow type."

She smiled and said, "Okay" and then walked with my dad out of the door. I could hear them talk but I couldn't make out what they were saying. It sounded ominous, though. Like one of those movies that starts off right, but takes a bad turn somewhere, about, right where I am.

Nurse May and my dad stopped talking and she walked back in and said, "Okay JJ, it seems you are fine so I am going to give you a little treatment in your IV and I will let you get some rest."

I answered, "I've already had my medicine today; what is this?" I asked because what she had in that needle was pink and I had never seen it before.

My dad came in and said, "Listen to the doctor, son. It will help you."

I gave a simple nod and she injected the pink stuff into my IV. I felt sleepy and my head fell back onto my pillow. Everything was blurry and the last thing I remembered was Nurse May leaning over and whispering in my ear, "Keep believing." I blacked out and woke up next day feeling no pain in my body.

A couple of days passed and the doctors said I was finally ready to go home. I still had a cast on my left arm, but they said it would come off in about a week or two. I was curious about Nurse May, looking for her as my dad and I walked out of the hospital, but I didn't seem to see her. As we approached the exit, I began to ask my dad about her, but I saw my mom running toward me. I held my peace because I didn't want my dad in trouble. My mother may not even know about her. I am given a small scolding by my mom on my way home, considering I didn't get one while I recovered.

Guess she wanted to make sure I was at full strength before I got it. She simply didn't want me to do reckless things anymore and wanted me to tell her every place I go and who I am hanging out with from then on. I simply nodded and listened all the way home until we pulled into the driveway.

My mother and father got out of the car but I stopped my dad and asked him to talk for a moment. He told my mother to go ahead and got back in the car. I maneuvered to the front and he asked me, "What is it, son?"

I replied, "Well Dad, I just wanted to know who Nurse May was."

My dad grinned and says "She is a nurse, son. What do you mean?"

"I mean I was looking for her on the way out and I didn't see her anywhere and almost every person who had something to do with me being in that hospital room saw me before I left except her."

My father gave me a serious look and answered, "She is someone I called in to see you. She is an old friend of the family and she is the best at what she does."

I looked at him bewildered and said, "Well what did you need her to see that the doctors didn't tell you already?"

He looked at me and said, "I wanted to see if there was some extra activity with your imagination for the stunt you pulled."

My heart jumped into my throat because one thing I couldn't afford was for my parents to put me in a looney bin because they think I am crazy. My dad continued, "But she said there is nothing more to be worried about, just a little boy who had an accident playing a game. A game I know he won't play again because I know he learned his lesson."

I responded with a small yes and he put his arms around me and said, "Son I want you to dream big but enough of this flight thing, okay? It is enough that you are so athletic now. Go out for football, or basketball, you know something you will excel in, but I want this dream of flight to stop. For your own safety, please stop with that dream."

I turned my head from him, stunned. I didn't know what to say. My father, the one who told me that if this dream is worth having, it's worth the trouble it takes, just told me to give up my dream. What do you do when the one who instilled in you "take the time and do it right" tells you to give up and do something else? It's not even something else that is important; it's something way below my standard. I didn't want to dribble a ball or throw the pigskin around; my dad had my little brother for that. I wanted the impossible; I wanted flight! And what did he mean "excel at something"? Didn't I just excel at healing? By the doctors' standard, I should have been in the hospital not moving, and the best-case scenario sitting in a wheelchair. Yet I walked like normal out of the hospital, I walked like normal to the car, I walked around to the front seat even without any trouble, and he wanted me to quit? I was speechless.

There lays a silence in the car while these thoughts run through my head. I think my dad is waiting for a response from me. I can't give him the one he wants because he will expect me to follow through and I can't cheat myself of flight; I said earlier that I refuse to be selfish but I would refuse to cheat myself out of what belongs to me. I still, however, feel my dad looking at me and as I go to give him the answer he wants to hear so I can get out of the car away from this atmosphere. I remember the voice of Nurse May. I heard her voice as if it is coming from the backseat of the car. "Keep believing." I have my answer for my dad. I simply tell him I will follow the nurse's order. He stares at me and then smiles, saying, "Good man."

There were several nurses that told me to take it easy and to be careful not to do the same thing again. My dad overheard them talking to me about this when I was getting ready to leave the hospital. But I was talking about the mysterious Nurse May's orders. It is almost like she knew this conversation would come up and rather than look a gift horse in the mouth again or ask more questions that could cause a major shift in my dad's demeanor—like what was that pink stuff she put in my IV, I simply say what he wants to hear and save the conversation for when I take flight and am at liberty to bring to the table any question I want.

We get out of the car and walked into the house up to my room smiling on the inside. Although I am a bit uneased about the over-active imagination card I think my dad threw at me to see if I would back off the flight thing. Yet, when I lay my head on my bed and feel no pain from the almost fatal accident I went through, I realize I am not crazy and I will keep following my dreams. After all, it's not in my best interest to disobey the doctor's orders, so I will keep on believing, even if I have to do it in private and in secret. This is more than wishful thinking; it is a dream that will come to pass.

Chapter 2

Hope Never Fails

I'm fifteen now and it has been three years since my little accident and my vow to follow the doctor's orders. "Keep believing," but I don't let my parents truly know what I am doing; although, my little sister Bella constantly tries to spy on me so she can find some type of dirt to get me with. Man, you think she'd have something better to do than follow me all over the place to get me in trouble.

My little brother Jackie is the most supportive of my dream of flight. He doesn't show it outwardly, but in our "bro time", he tells me that he sometimes wishes he was like me.

My father goes on and on about sports like it's the pinnacle of greatness, so in order to get his approval, my brother plays football for our school and he goes at it hard. I mean, he keeps coming close to breaking each school record, but he chokes every time. I think he may be afraid to believe in himself because of me and my flight dreams. After all, my parents still do think I'm a little off my rocker.

After my accident three years ago I found Roy, Mark, and John for my parkour training. It was the hardest thing to do—not because it was hard to locate them, but because my mother refused to let me out of her sight whenever I went running. To make matters worse, whenever she couldn't be around me, she would send my brother or sister. Thankfully, she didn't know about my brother's secret approval because he became cool with Roy and the gang.

I found out it was Mark who called the ambulance when I fell into the dumpster after they took me on that trial run. Man, my brother was so mad, he tried to fight all three of them for leaving me like they did on that run. Although Mark called the ambulance, he didn't stay too close when they arrived because they thought they would get in trouble for egging me on like they did. I don't blame him though—I was the one on the roof and I was the one who made the jump so foolishly.

My brother, however, didn't see it that way and it took everything I had to keep him from taking them on. Even before my brother got into football, he always had a natural strength about him that could possibly rival a grown man. If it wasn't for the fact that I worked out so much at the time, I don't think I would have been able to hold him back.

Since Roy reluctantly admitted to leaving me for dead, he agreed to train me the right way so I would be at least be able to roll on the ground without scratching myself up. For the first few months, my brother trained with me because he didn't trust the PG or Parkour Gang, that's what I call them. John told me that if I ever gave them a corny nickname like that again, he would leave me in another dumpster somewhere, and my brother agreed. That's when he started trusting them and leaving me with them to pursue my dream. When you can get Jackie to laugh and be sincere about his laugh, you have earned his trust.

Up until my thirteenth birthday, Roy constantly threatened to leave me if I didn't catch up and get the tricks and tactics he tried to show me. Unbeknownst to him, I practiced until I met up with him for our daily workouts and all the way home until I got under the watchful eye of my family. I would always come back doing what he showed me even better than Mark and John. The training would be like a friendly competition between the four of us and once I was able to hold my own with them when we competed, we competed. Talk about intense—it was constant running, wall running, flips, and rolling. They even knew some competent self-defense techniques that allowed them to keep up with my karate and boxing.

I know not to underestimate anyone anymore—especially Mark. Man, talk about a one-man army. I was able to outrun him but I was barely able to land a punch on him when sparring. His hands were like superhuman fast. He knew win-chun punching techniques that allowed him to punch three punches per second! Not joking. One time, we spared so bad that I went home with two black eyes and he went home with a smile. Try to explain to your already overprotective, oversensitive, and over-paranoid mom why you have two black eyes. I just told her an old friend and I had a disagreement over who was better and then I found myself under the radar—this time by the snitch Bella.

Although I never let Bella meet my friends, she would occasionally see me talking with them on my way home from school. Immediately she would run up to see who they were but they would leave before she arrived. I stressed to them that she could not see them run up the walls of the nearby building or that was the end of the Parkour four. I haven't said that out loud to John; he may not be the best fighter, but he is definitely an aggressive one. He doesn't like bad nicknames. I called him "quacker back" one time and he chased me halfway home with a dirty rag claiming he would clean my mouth out of all bad jokes.

Unfortunately, the third month of my fourteenth year, I had to limit, if not at all stop, the time that I hung out with them. It is not like I had become so good that I didn't need them because no one is so good that they don't need help. For me, even if I was that good, I would still hold on to them, for they became great friends, but not even all friends understand the wildest of dreams. You know, it's funny. I thought my brother or sister would rat me out to my parents and they would tell me to stop hanging out with my buddies, but they didn't. Roy was the one who ended the bonds we had.

One day, after a run, we sat down and decided to rest and were talking and joking around about nothing, when we started talking about dreams. Roy said he wanted to be the best Parkour runner ever. Everyone looked at him without shock because it was apparent that's what his goal was. I mean, this man will run from sun up to sun down if he could. I know because I looked out my window one night when I couldn't sleep and saw him running on houses around my block. I believe he woke up Mr. Johansson when he landed on the roof of his house roughly and had to hurry and run away because Mr. Johansson keeps a shotgun handy for anyone dumb enough to try to break into his house.

Mark's dream did surprise us, however, when he told us that he wanted to be a stockbroker and yes, the guy is smart, but to have the patience and intelligence to deal with numbers all day is way beyond me.

John's dream was simple and nothing exciting; he wants to be a chef at a restaurant called the Golden Crab. It's a restaurant downtown that all the rich folks go to. When we asked why he wanted a job like that, he grew serious and said his dad worked there and he was the best. He was determined to be a lot like his dad, who had suffered a stroke and was now confined to a wheelchair. I personally thought that he could do better with all his skill as a runner, but who am I to judge another man's dream.

When it was my turn, however, I was not only hesitant to tell them that I wanted to fly, but now, looking back on it, part of me wishes I hadn't said anything at all. Maybe I should have made something up or maybe I should have changed the subject or I could have cut the break short to see if they would have forgotten the whole conversation, but I thought, *what's the point of having a dream if you can't share it with your friends?* So I told them that I wanted to fly and right away, they thought I meant airplane pilot or Air Force pilot, or even create a new flying invention. I corrected them and said, "No I mean I actually want to fly myself."

They all laughed, thinking I was joking. Mark even threw a crack at me, telling me not to smoke weed right before running because the weed would take the first fifty percent of my oxygen and the run would take the last fifty out of me. As time passed, and I sat still with a straight face and it dawned on them that I was serious about my flight and that the first words I spoke to Roy were, "I want to fly and you guys are my ticket." With shocked faces, no one said anything.

We must have sat for an hour before Roy got up and said, "Let's call it a day, fellas." They went in one direction and me, with great stress, headed home. I had made it home in time for dinner and I could barely eat. My mother was worried and I assured her that I would be all right. My brother came up to check on me after I had left the dinner table, but I told him I would be fine as well.

That night went by like months on a calendar as I lay in my bed, wondering what Roy and the gang thought about my ambition. Were they thinking that I was a nut case? Could they have thought how stupid I was for believing such a thing, or how stupid they were for not believing me when I first told them what I wanted to do? I couldn't let that bother me. I mean, these guys are my friends; they may have left me in a dumpster to die once, but they also called the ambulance and taught me Parkour. Every day after my stay in the hospital was filled with hope and fun because of the bond I created with the PG's. I was on my way to flight, already feeling like I was flying parkouring all over the place and making jumps across alleyways and down fire escapes that I wouldn't dare make before. As an added plus, I made new friends along the way.

I haven't had a lot of friends because of this journey that I am on. I told you before that I had not just taken up gymnastics, but boxing and karate because I was picked on so much after I stood in front of the class one day in third grade and said I wanted to fly. I couldn't tell you the number of swirleys, bumps, bruises, and black eyes I got from bigger kids who thought I was better than them for wanting such a thing, or even stupid for thinking I could attain such a thing.

Then, one day, my dad had had enough and enrolled me in boxing and it wasn't long before I went to school looking for the same kids who put my head in the toilet, trying to drown me and my dream. I only took karate because they had exercises that would have helped strengthen my legs and teach me how to kick for the occasional bully who knew a little boxing. But that was a long time ago I'm not bullied anymore, and I am not friendless anymore, and now I realize it's time to go to sleep because stressing over this won't help me and worrying about what my friends are thinking will not help either. I had a feeling everything was going to be all right.

The next day had come and I went to our original meeting place to see if they guys were there getting ready to go for a run. I went but I didn't see anybody, so I figured I was early and I began to stretch out my body for the day. I had to have waited for an hour and still, no show from the guys. I didn't wait too much longer before I went looking for them around our run spots. With the skill I now possessed, it wasn't hard for me to get where I needed to go— after all, Parkour is the fastest way between two points. As I went on my mission, searching for my companions, I was amazed at how far I had come from not knowing how to roll, right to jumping from rooftop to rooftop. I guess I was so busy learning from Roy, Mark, and John that I never stopped to evaluate my progress, but of course, Mark always told me while he was teaching me that it's not always about being serious, it's about having fun.

I was always trying so hard to catch up to where the others were I hadn't stopped to realize I had caught up and I was doing a great job at parkour by myself. The exhilaration I felt along with the adrenaline and endorphin flow throughout my body was unreal. I found myself pushing harder to see how far I could go, but I stopped and reminded myself of my little accident and that I wouldn't go down that road again. Besides that, I reminded myself I was looking for my friends whom I had just found a rooftop away, looking in the opposite direction of me. I stopped just short of the edge of the rooftop and started walking slowly to them when they turned and saw me approach. I wanted to say, "What's up guys," but there was a solemn look in their eyes that alarmed me greatly.

Here I was, on one roof, and there they were on another, and it felt like we could've been miles away from each other. I took notice of their position on the roof and saw they had a perfect view of the neighborhood. I ran across all of it to get where I was, so there was no doubt that they saw me on my run.

Mark was the first to leave the rooftop, jumping down from the steep ledge only saying, "Later little pilot." John was the second to go, as he gave me a head nod and smirk following Mark's lead. Then the one who welcomed me into the group only stood looking at me said, "What are you chasing us so hard for?"

It was then I realized I had what I needed from them; my skill had improved so much since we met that I didn't need them to teach me anything else. Like I said, they were my friends I wanted to hang on to them, so I chased after them. They were more than teachers; they were a part of my life. Did I have to let them go because I wanted to fly so bad, or could I make up some story that let them know I was just joking?

Then it dawned on me that this was another roof trial. Do I compromise like my dad wanted me to and come down from this height, or do I push myself and excel beyond what I think I can do and make this leap without the PGs? Roy still looked at me, waiting for an answer. I gave him one: "I needed to know how to run before I could fly."

He smirked and jumped down the steep ledge. I ran several paces away from the ledge before blasting off full force into a high jump onto the other roof and this time, unlike the first time, I made my jump. I made progress and with tears in my eyes, I made my way home doing every trick Roy, Mark, and John showed me, kind of a memorial to the friendship we shared.

I still, to this day, don't know if they thought I was crazy or not, but what I do know is they can't think I am too crazy because every now and then, I see them on their run while I'm on mine. And the few times our paths cross, they let me in on the exercise and as we run to our old rest spots and they trail off to one direction and I trail off on my own. I know it's not in vain, losing my running buddies. I mean, my little brother checks up on me to make sure I'm okay. He still gets a little upset when he thinks about how they stopped hanging out with me for telling them that I wanted to fly. He always says, "They are jumping around town like maniacs and they want to judge you for wanting to fly?! Are you kidding me, man?! I better not run into them or I will knock 'em straight into the sky! That will show them flight is for real!"

He may be a little violent but at least he gets me to laugh.

I know running now may be a little bittersweet at times, but it will be worth when I am up in the air, soaring through the sky. I'm practically doing it now; I just have to come back to Earth for a small break. Remember, I'm doing this the right way, not the rushed way, and I feel like I'm closer than I think to my dream coming true.

Chapter 3

Dream Killer

So, I have had some ups and downs before, but today had to be the worst day of my life. I went to school like normal, and I was ready to follow through with my plan like every other day. Get up at six o'clock and do sixty-five push-ups, take a shower, eat breakfast, and be out the door by seven-thirty. Go to school and maintain my school grades so that I can keep Mom and Dad off my back while I pursue my dream as well as duck and dodge my little sister so I can avoid agitation while I am training. Hang out with my little brother after his football practice and see how things are going with him because he is having a hard time in physics. Go home and eat dinner like a "regular, normal, everyday, average family." Seems simple enough, right? Wrong! With every plan there comes a possibility of interruptions and today, mine was Tony Daemon, the ninth grade bully.

It all started in between periods when I was leaving math to go to PE when Tony started following me and making fun of me for wearing a leotard in the seventh grade. Man, everyone else who went to my old school has forgotten about that, except this guy. I swear it's the only funny material that he has and yes, he gets a few chuckles out of the other students who don't know me, but even they get tired of it. Tony belabors the point so much that it becomes the complete opposite of funny. It like he is crying out for attention and going after anyone who is different from the crowd. It's funny — I thought we left bullies in grade school, but apparently, some people are so insecure about themselves that they have to make others feel worse so they can feel good for at least an hour. Mind you, I said all of this to Tony and before I knew it, he blackened my eye. All I could see as I lay on the ground for those five seconds were stars.

Don't think for a second I took that cheap shot lying down (no pun intended). I got up and began wailing on him to show him that gymnastics was not the only thing I practiced. I showed great skill in slipping and dodging every punch he threw at me and with whatever force he gave, I gave back twice as much. Truthfully, it was nowhere near a fair fight. I mean, Tony was winded within the first minute. He may have muscle, but he is sorely lacking in stamina and endurance. So it's easy to catch him off balance and punish him for it. This was so easy, I stopped and tried to walk away. I mean, there is no challenge and by this time, I'd beaten him so bad that I might get expelled for a fight that I didn't even start.

As I walked away from him to pick up my bags, I made the fatal mistake of turning my back on someone who wasn't ready to call it quits. I felt two big bulky arms grab me around my waist and lift me into the air onto my back and neck. I had a quick flashback of when I fell in that dumpster and I remembered the amount of pain I was in and was quickly filled with rage. That was my second mistake—getting so mad that I got up and unleashed the full force of my fury on this would-be tough guy. John, one of the PGs, once told me that it's never good to get so upset that you could become blind. You could either hurt someone, someone could hurt you, or worse—you could hurt yourself. Too bad for Tony. Today it was him and I paid the price for it.

I was in the principal's office between two security guards, waiting for my mom and dad to get to the school to hear the principal and my homeroom teacher talk bad about me. The principal had nothing on me, except he caught me running on the walls of the hallway one day. He told me to never do it again and I haven't, at least not in school. It was the homeroom teacher, Mr. Walker, who's the dream killer and believe me—not just me, the whole school thinks so. The principal piggybacks off of what he says most of the time. In Mr. Walker's eyes, unless you come from an upstart family with a lot of money to fall back on, you will be nothing but an average class, working individual. Notice I said *individual*, not citizen, because citizens do something to help their country and community, and in his eyes, that's not me. And heaven help you if you have an awe-inspiring goal and he knows about it. He will do everything in his power to get you to think "realistically" and within your means. He has done nothing but sway several of my classmates to downgrade themselves to nine through five jobs, making ten dollars an hour.

Even this cute girl in my class named Kate—she wanted to be the first fashion model who didn't take off her clothes to get to the top. And truth be told, she had the body to pull it off, but it's not her body that gets my attention, it's her eyes and how blue they are. One time I saw her at night while coming home from working out and I just happened to pass her while the moon was fully lit and it's amazing how gorgeous those blue sapphires looked in that great moonlight.

She mistakenly told the dream killer what she wanted to do and he did nothing but outright laugh in her face in front of all the students. He told her she was better off walking on water. I could have said a long time ago there was this one instance when one person successfully did it. Two people, to be precise, but unless you can present facts to this man like cold hard cash and a family name that half the world knows, then it's no use arguing with him. After class, she looked like her whole life's purpose had just been crushed and the dream killer stood looking at her like he wanted to hear her say, "I will get a real job." It's almost like when my dad was looking at me, trying to get me to give up my dreams and I wasn't about to let that happen. I took it upon myself to do what a still-mysterious nurse did for me and so I walked up to her in his presence and said out loud, "Keep believing." The fire I saw in this man's eye was unquenchable. I have made it my mission that whenever I am in his class to openly defy him about the impossible. He has tried several times to take a shot at my dream of flight, the only reason he knows about it is from Tony and how he heard me say it in the fifth grade. Yet, with all his reason and logic, I still when our debates with a simple response: "Well whatever I succeed or fail at I will have more hair on my head than you." He has a poor combover, so that gets him every time.

This time he may actually win against me because the one thing my mother hates more than me hurting myself in my pursuits is fighting. Her saying is, "You better have had no other option and even if it was your last option, you're still grounded when you get home because fighting leads nowhere except to the grave." Man, my mother is so loving at times but other times she can be beyond reason.

My mother and father walk into the office shocked to see my eye black, wondering where the kid I was fighting was. My mother rushed over to hug me and kissed me, embarrassing me at the same time. My father walked over and examined my eye, probably making sure I didn't have to go to the hospital.

The dream killer interrupted my mother hugging and said, "If you are looking for the other young man, he is on a stretcher on his way to the hospital."

My mother replied, "To the hospital? What for?"

His tone to my mother was so snobby, it was ridiculous. "Your son bruised several of his ribs, broke his nose, and blackened both of his eyes."

My father chimed in and asked me if that is true. I replied with a simple, "Yes."

Both of my parents were stunned and as I began to explain why, I was rudely interrupted by the dream killer as he went on a rant and rave. "Your son is openly disrespectful, arrogant, and that nice boy deserved nothing that he got!"

I responded with anger in my voice and said, "Well why didn't he deserve the beating I gave him? Because he is the dream killer junior? He punched me in my eye and slammed me on back and neck after I tried to walk away. He attacked me for calling him out on being someone who has nothing better to do but belittle others so that he could feel good about himself and come to think of it, that sounds an awful lot like you!"

I was stopped by mother and told to be respectful, although she was fully aware of my anger and frustration.

Then, when I think my little outburst has put Mr. Walker in his place, he blasts out my dream in front of my mother and father. Now, normally this wouldn't be a problem if they already knew I was still pursuing it, but they honestly thought I had stopped.

Mr. Walker went on to say, "It is your son's childish active imagination that has caused an uproar in my class and amongst the students. He honestly thinks he can fly!"

My throat sunk into my chest as my father looked at me with shock and my mother looked at me with awe. You know, the bad kind of awe like, "I can't believe this is happening."

Mr. Walker didn't stop there. Apparently he's a stalker and has seen me with the PGs. "Your son hangs out with the most reckless group of kids around town. They jump on roofs, run on the walls, and even scale buildings like a bunch of circus freaks. Young Jason has constantly put himself at risk with these escapades so I don't blame Tony or myself for trying to talk some sense into him so he can actually graduate on time with a proper head on his shoulders. He has even been caught running on the walls here in school."

The principal chimed in, "Yes Mr. and Mrs. Parker, it's true. I have had to tell him to stop."

Those are the only words that come out of his mouth the entire meeting and yet they are more than enough to help bury me as my father looked at me with rage in his eyes while my mother's eyes filled with tears.

I looked angrily at Mr. Walker, the dream killer, and he had the audacity to smirk at me as if to say, "Checkmate." There was silence for several moments when my father asked for the punishment for the fight. The principal gave me four days' suspension. When I tried to protest to ask how many days the one who started the fight will get, I was stopped by my mother. I was walked out of the office by my mother and father and escorted to my locker and teachers to gather my belongings and assignments for the four days. Kate caught a glimpse of me as I left the building and ran to me, asking if I was okay. I responded with a "yes" but not even these blue eyes could help soften the blows that awaited me in the car ride ahead. She tried to talk a little, but my father interrupted her and told me to get in the car.

The car ride home is mostly in silence. I heard a couple of sniffles from my mom and nothing but labored breathing from my dad. They probably thought a thousand and one thoughts concerning me and I dared not imagine what was going through their heads. I might imagine too well and get exactly what I think or I may underestimate and get more than what I bargained for.

We pulled into the driveway and headed straight to the kitchen. The kitchen in our house was like the interrogation room and because my brother and sister were still at school we had no unwarranted interruptions. My sister wasn't around to be nosey and my brother wasn't there to come up with some excuse for me.

My mother started with, "How could you still be doing this? Don't you realize what danger you put yourself in or the harm you could cause yourself? It's one thing to be doing these stunts because you may want to make a profession out of it, but to do it because you think you can actually fly is getting to be too much. You can't fly, baby. It's time to let that dream go now."

Before I could say anything, my dad went off on me with a tone in his voice that could shatter a mountain. "Never mind the dream! How about how you told me that this would end? How about how you told me that you would follow the doctor's orders and stop?! Yet you boldly lied to me about what you were going to do. You lied to me about what you were doing all the time. We thought you were going running when you actually found those nuts who I think had something to do with putting you in the hospital in the first place! You have no privileges; do you understand me? None whatsoever; you cannot go out for running, you cannot go out for exercise and when you do go out, it will be with your sister, since apparently, you are able to duck and dodge your brother. Or maybe your brother had something to do with you hanging out with them. I don't know, but what I do know is I will deal with him when he gets home. This is over! Do you understand me? Over! Last time I gave you a choice, but this time it's not happening."

At that point, I could have pulled the Nurse May card. At that point, I could've asked what the pink stuff was that was put in my IV. At that point, I could've turned the barrel of my mother against my father and put him on the spot. But I didn't. I don't know why, but I didn't. I promised myself never to be selfish and put my family through pain because of my dream. So I didn't throw my dad under the bus in order to save something that didn't need saving. But what I was not about to do was throw away my goal. So I stood staring at him letting him know this wasn't the end and I was far from giving up. I have had obstacles before and I have overcome them. Me falling and breaking almost every bone in my body, losing my friends the PGs, the fight with Tony, and even the verbal bout with Mr. Walker. This is nothing different.

We stared at each other for hours when my mother broke the silence and told me to go to my room. I walked out respectfully to keep the tension down and as I entered my room, tears began to roll down my face as I lay on my bed. When the day first began, I thought there was just one dream killer, but as I lay crying, I feel like the world is full of them and some of them live in your very own home. Parents who want you to do your best, but don't want you to shoot for the impossible because they see it as impossible. Teachers who teach for paychecks alone and not to truly impart something to those who will go off and shape the future of the world. And bullies to afraid to dream so much so that they pull you down to their level and suffocate your dreams with fear and intimidation. It was one thing to fight one or two of them, but the whole world? Who am I to even hope to win? Then it dawned on me. Who am I to think I can fly? If I can come so close to this dream, then surely I can beat a world full of doubters. I just have to do it, one battle at a time.

Later, about three o' clock, my brother came in with a disgruntled look on his face. I think he wanted to punch me, but he just looked at me and asked me if I won. I smirked for the first time that day and said, "Yeah, I won."

Jackie was not as upset. He told me about the butt ripping Dad just landed him about not telling him about the PG's. He, however, is not grounded like I am (no pun intended). My dad was probably so mad at me that he couldn't punish my little brother.

Now my day had started to get better, but when my little sister kicked in my door things got worse.

My sister Bella stood and smiled at me and my brother, before saying, "How was your day, big loveable brother?" Mind you, she talked with my parents before she came up here to my room. She continued, "Well, my day was fine, although yours was not. But I know some news that will brighten up all of our days. For the next four days, whenever you have anywhere to go, I am coming with you."

As if that wasn't bad enough, she started to rub it in and act like a drill sergeant. When we were little, my dad would always tell us stories about when he first went into the service and how the drill sergeants were. Those stories apparently stuck because she picked up the attitude well.

"All right, maggot, we get up at o six hundred! You will not eat, sleep, or scratch your butt without my say-so, is that understood?"

Before I could get up and rip her a new one for being a brat, my mother came in and told my sister that that was enough. My mother was not in the mood to be played with and my little sister went to her room. My mother directed my brother to his room and closed the door to talk to me.

She started with my punishments and restrictions, and what I am and I am not allowed to do.

After which, she talked to me in the calmest of tones ever. "Son," she said, "I want you to be on your best behavior. No more lying, no going where you are not supposed to go. I want you to know that I will always love you whether you want to be a fireman or police officer. And I know you don't want to hear this, but I am asking you to think rationally for once and give this up. You are breaking my heart because I am starting to think . . ."

She didn't finish that statement, but I knew where she was going with that. Unlike my dad right now, who doesn't want to hear anything about flight, I can talk to my mom.

I simply said to her, "Momma, I want you to know I love you too, but I cannot and will not give this up. Men are capable of doing great things and none of those people would have done those things if they had listened to the nay-sayers around them. They were all told that their dreams were impossible, but look, we have cars now; we have a knowledge of the microscopic world, which enables us to create revolutionary medicines. And my favorite example is the Wright Brothers. The men who created flying machines and now we are flying to the moon and beyond. Why should this be any different? I am sorry, but I will not give this up until my feet leave the ground and I soar through the air."

With a hurt expression on her face, she left the room and closed the door behind her. And that made it official; when you can hurt your mother, that becomes the worst day of your life.

Chapter 4

Yet I Jump Higher Everyday

T wo days after my suspension and life in this house had become like a prison. I can't watch TV or play video games. I can use my computer only to do homework, so social media is out, not that I had many friends on it anyway. Whenever I go to the store, Bella comes along and she is a pest every step of the way. On the first day, when my mother sent me to the east side market, my sister came with me and egged me on to do a wall run because she had never seen it before. So I thought, *why not. Maybe she is serious about this and it would be a good exercise for me.* I wall ran from one building to the next and when we got home, she snitched on me! My dad gave me another lecture about how a man is supposed to be a man of his word. After that, I didn't trust the little girl anymore. Fool me once, shame on you, fool me twice, shame on me. Whenever we go out, she runs ahead of me to try and get me to run. I take my slow time and walk—after all, it's the only air I get anyway.

Today is the third day that I have been suspended and it has not taken long before I was able to make a routine out of my day. In the morning I wake up and get dressed to take my sister to school. I am met by my mother on the way home to make sure I don't take a side trip. I return home to do my schoolwork before cleaning the house from top to bottom. I am made to do this because my parents are trying to make sure I am too exhausted to do any type of exercise. I am, however, filled with energy once I start cleaning and while I clean, I think about how to run better and how to breathe better. They can trap my body in this house, but my mind is another game; you can't touch that.

I am always done with cleaning by the end of twelve o' clock. So most of the time I lay around until my mother goes off to work at the staffing agency. She only works part-time for extra cash because my father's job is sufficient to take care of all the expenses. He is a stockbroker and he is good at what he does because he just got another bonus. I hope he doesn't want me to do that with my life because I may have to disappoint him.

When my mother leaves for work, I do push-ups and sit ups to stay in shape. I know it's only been two days and I haven't been in the house too long, but for someone who needs and loves to be outside to train, this is killing me. I have too much energy and too many new tricks and tactics I need to try in order to fly. Once, on the first day, I thought about maybe sneaking out but my dad has tasked one of my neighbors to watch the house when they are not there in order to make sure I don't pull anything. Plus, it would hurt my mom to do something like that so I decided against it.

One thing I have done to keep cool, calm, and collected is meditating on the sky. John once told me that you have to be patient with yourself if you want to go far in the Parkour game, so he taught me to meditate so I could be patient and learn how to sit still after I had worked out my muscles to their max.

I do nothing but sit still and think of everything I've done and everything I could still do in order to fly. When I sit and think like this, it is like I am in a bubble and time becomes irrelevant. I think a thousand thoughts in only a matter of seconds and my world is uninterrupted by my brother, sister, mother, or father. I am in my own world and you have no access unless I grant it. It's interesting how people say some things in the world are impossible, but I see there is nothing impossible, especially now when I recognize I am sitting here, allowing time to flow over me like water over a stone and I'm not bothered by the constant interruptions that may await a man. I smirk and say to myself, "Impossible. Yeah right."

The mind is the key to being different in your environment. When you have a made up mind, you can do anything you set your mind to. A man can have drugs all around him, but if he doesn't want to do it and has his mind made up that he won't do it, he won't do it. If a man is hurt, but is determined not to let that hurt stop him from living, he will do it if his mind is made up. I knew a boy who was wronged by his family member in which he had all his money stolen from him. The boy, however, was determined not to be a thief because someone had stolen from him. It's a mind thing and my mind is made up that no matter where I am held up, I will find a way to get into the air and fly without the aid of a machine.

It's now the third day and I want to do more than just think today, so I have decided to start journaling to keep up with my progress. I know it's something that I haven't committed to doing before but that's because I was always on the move, improving my physical capabilities and not ever wanting to sit still long enough to write. In school, my writing teacher Mrs. Caring would have the hardest time with me, not because I was being purposely disruptive, but because I had so much energy sometimes that I would even be hot in my body. She was smart and enthusiastic though, not like the dream killer Mr. Walker. Man, I can't stand him but I am not about to think about him. Mrs. Caring had a way of using the students' energy and distractions as a tool to help them learn and be better. Since I had such a hard time sitting still, she used the one thing that got my attention to help me write and sit still: flying. She suggested I write stories about flying and how I would use it to help others. One time, she even suggested I write a to-do list of what I would do first when I was able to fly. I must admit I'm pretty good at writing right now because of her. She didn't think I was weird or crazy like my other teachers; she thought I was unique, optimistic, and hopeful.

She came to me once and said: "I wish the world had more dreamers like you; it would make the world a better place."

One thing I miss about school right now is her; her class is always warm and welcoming. Maybe I could be a writer if the flight doesn't work out. No! I am not giving up on flying. It will work out and I can still be a writer when it happens. Take that, Mr. Walker; number one overachiever right here!

So I journal a little before my dad gets home. He was always the first one out of the door and the last one to get home because of his work. I admired that about him, how he would sacrifice his time for us so that we could have the best and the best opportunities presented to us. But now he has been taking off early to get home, no doubt to check on me.

My journal entries are not super scientific or anything; they are simple and straight to the point.

Journal Entry 1: Have not run today, let alone flown, because of my strict punishment. Mediation time was fruitful and I have new ideas about how to get into the air. Later's much."

I keep my entries vague just in case my family gets a hold of it. I am not being interrogated again like some criminal because I want to keep trying to fly. It's possible I just know it is and lately, my stomach has had this warm feeling in it and some days it gets hot. I have checked myself to make sure I'm not sick or have the stomach flu, but I am fine. I even had my mother check me and she told me I am fit as a horse. I try not to think about it much but now I can hear my dad calling me downstairs so I go to see what he wants. When I get there, he tells me to sit down on the couch across from him. We haven't talked much since I came home from school and was grounded.

I am waiting for him to say something to me because we have been sitting for several moments and then the silence is broken. "Son," my dad says, "I want to know why you want to fly so bad. I know it's something that you wanted to do as a child, but all children have that dream at least once. They eventually give it up and go on to something else; why haven't you?"

I respond and say, "Dad, I want to fly because I believe I was put here to fly. This isn't just a dream to me. It's a goal, it's a must-have in my life and I won't stop until it is mine." With a look of disappointment, he tells me that my mother told him what I said several days ago. He expresses how he was displeased with the tears in her eyes and how I hurt her. That was the last straw; it's like he uses these incidents to get me in my place, but me hurting my mother especially when I didn't intend to was too far.

"Does mom know about the nurse who put the pink stuff in my IV when I was twelve?" The shock and anger I see on his face are apparent.

"Boy, are you trying to be smart or blackmail me?"

I answer, "No I am trying to put all of this together. Why can't I attain the impossible and why is the one who told me I could do anything telling me now that I can't?" He is stunned and simply tells me to go to my room until my mother gets home.

My mother returns home and even then I don't leave my room. I am boiling mad at my father and instead of being disrespectful, I stay there until my brother and sister get home. Jackie comes up to calm me down and tells me to always be respectful to our parents. Most of the time he looks up to me but there are those rare occasions that he gives advice to me which helps me out a lot. At dinner time we go downstairs to eat but the tension at the dinner table is so thick that we can hardly digest our food. My dad refuses to look at me and I am not anxious to return a gaze. This is by far the longest dinner night of all of our lives.

The last day of my suspension is different than the other three days. I actually slept in and was not awaken by my mother or father. I go downstairs to see if anyone is home and everybody is gone. My mother left a note on the refrigerator that said, "Wanted to get you some rest today. You have school tomorrow so be ready and behave yourself. For some reason, however, your father has lifted some of your punishments but we would appreciate it if you didn't leave the house until one of us got home so we could talk about. I left breakfast in the microwave. Love, Momma."

Whoa! This cannot be real because never in my parents' life have they ever lifted off a punishment of me and my brother. My sister, yeah, but you know she is the favorite. My father is a kind but strict police officer and my mother don't believe in parole so this is a shock to me. I, however, don't want to push it so I do stay home and watch some TV until my mother gets there.

When she walks in the door, something about her mood has changed. I don't know what it is, but it's a little uneasy and I'm waiting for her to tell me to turn the TV off so she could talk to me. She does not however and leaves me to the television. Maybe she would rather see me watching TV like a normal teenager than wall running; at this point, I really can't blame her. We as a family have been through a lot by this point. The day goes on and like clockwork, my brother comes through the door making a crack at me.

He says, "Glad to see you out on probation inmate."

Whatever man, he is always making little jokes to lighten the mood. And then comes my sister who is displeased to me see watching TV before her. She has only had to share it with my brother for the last three days so this comes as a major interruption to her. She calls for my mom and tries to tell on me.

My mother simply says, "Leave that boy alone and go play in your room." Again, that uneased me because she does not take Bella's side like she normally would.

Last but not least, my father walks in and sees me laying on the couch. I had decided not to go out before both of my parents got home so that I could avoid any further trouble. He simply looks at me and says, "Is there anything good on?"

I reply, "Well Sanford and Sons is on and some cruddy cartoons but other than that, no."

My father sits down next to me and asks, "Mind if I join you?"

I reply with "No I don't mind." I guess at this point everyone in the house just wanted things to go back to normal because here we are, sitting here, and neither one us says a thing about yesterday. Well, I guess it's best not to look a gift horse in the mouth. It's not often I sit with my dad in peace not because he was always getting on my case about doing something productive with my life because I was. It was because I was afraid to sit next to him and talk to him in fear that he might find out that I am pursuing my dream. He had a presence about him that let me, my brother, and sister know that we could open up to him but I didn't want to open up to him about that because he didn't accept what I wanted to do. And he was not crazy about the dangers that came along with it either, because of the simple fact I ended up in a dumpster. I guess I wouldn't want my kid doing something so dangerous either if I had a child.

My father breaks the silence and starts to tell me about what I am allowed to do and what I can't do. Before he can get into it, my mother hurries in from the kitchen and tells me to go to the east side marketplace for some tomatoes and a fresh apple. I look to my dad for approval because I don't want him to think that I am going to get away from this talk.

He nods and says, "Go ahead and do what your mother says, son. We will talk when you get back."

I go off on the porch and wait for my little sister to come but my mother comes out to tells me to go on ahead and to hurry back. I go with haste so the little tattletale can't catch up with me.

I waste no time in running to the east side market. On the way, there is nothing but alleyways and fire escapes that lead to small buildings. I'm trying not to push my freedom but I can't help it that burning feeling in my stomach is back and now it's stronger than ever. It's like it came to keep me from passing up this opportunity and the compulsion is too strong. I can't ignore it. The first wall I see I hit a wall run that leads to a long jump and then a roll onto the ground. Man, that felt great! The next alley I see, I can't resist. I see several fire escapes that lead to the next building and it's only a block away from the market. Well, it's been said that the fastest way to get between two points is parkour and that's how I will get home before my mom or dad sends Bella for me and she ends my runner's high. The jump to the rail is simple and as I make my way to the other escape, I push off with all the strength in my legs and make it. It's funny, but that fire escape was far, even for the most experienced, but I made it with no sweat. I won't worry about that now.

I make my way all the way to the roof and I have a great view of the east side market. The store my mother wants me to go to is David's Dell, it's the place where we get all our veggies because they are the best grown. He wins the gardening competition every year.

The marketplace looks pretty and colorful because the harvest festival is held here every year and every year my family is here, eating all the organic food snacks we can get our hands on. I see wires that hold the festival lights attached to the building I'm on to the store next to David's Dell. I run and jump down onto it using my gymnastic skills and I start swinging on it, making my way down to the store. I didn't have time to show off like I wanted to because I didn't need anyone to see me and report my actions back to my mother. Come to think of it, I didn't think about jumping on that wire; it just happened out of reflex. That's odd because I love free running, but I never do anything without thinking it through. Well, I'm not about to stress it now; time to get those tomatoes and apple.

I make my way to the store and I say hello to Mr. David, the store owner.

He says, "Hello young dreamer. I can't call ya little any more cause you're almost bigger than me!" He is always saying he is five-foot-four I have been bigger than him since I was fourteen years old. "Well, what can I do you for, little man? More of that organic energy juice you always chugging down?"

His funny accent always makes me laugh, but I say to him with a smile on my face, "No. I need a couple of tomatoes and an apple for my mother. Do you have any left?"

He replies, "Well shucks, young man. I told your ma this morning I was fresh out until after the festival. I can't grow 'em that fast."

I look at him bewildered wondering why my mother sent me down here. This makes me uneasy, so I make my way home. I tell Mr. David thanks and sorry for the confusion and then exit his store.

Before I go home, I go to the park that's several blocks down in the opposite direction of home and put my legs on the rails to do some handstand push-ups to help me think. I'm thinking about why my mother sent me there if she had already been there. Was she trying to get me out of the house so I could avoid another talk with Dad or did she just need to talk to Dad while I wasn't around? I put my legs down and begin to make my home before she starts to worry.

Before I can truly start, I hear Bella calling me. Man, I wasn't even gone that long even with this short rest. My dad must have sent her to make sure I didn't lollygag. As I begin to make my way to her, she says something to me that relights that fire I felt in my belly before. She says, "Hurry up and come home! You can't fly anyway!"

That tears it. I blast off into a strong sprint and as I pass David's Dell, I leap high into the air in an attempt to touch the sign he has in his store. Without a wall run or boost, it's impossible to reach, but something amazingly scary happens. I leap, but I leap so high that I not only touch the sign I knock it off of the building. And for a second, I felt like gravity had truly lost its hold on me and I was free from the thing that would pull me back down to the ground.

As I realize what has happened, I feel gravity take hold of me again and I come down several feet away from the Dell. I look back to see the sign I knocked down and cannot believe what just happened. Maybe not believing is why I came back down and gravity was allowed to take hold of me again, but before I could ponder too much, Mr. David comes out and screams, "What in tarnation happened?"

I try to explain I knocked down when I jumped up to touch it, but he doesn't believe me and blames it on the PGs who he sees me hanging around with. He thinks I'm trying to protect them and dismisses everything I say and goes on a rant: "When I catch those crazy circus clowns I'm a make 'em fix it and I'm a put 'em out in the garden to grow the towns food for a month to learn 'em some real work ethic."

Mr. David pushes for me to go home and I walk up to my sister, who missed the whole thing! She had turned her back on me after she had finished taunting. Finally, this was the moment that I needed to prove to her and my family that I wasn't crazy. As big as her mouth is, she wouldn't be able to help but to tell the house and half the block. As we walk home, I find it hard to be discouraged because she missed the dawning of a miraculous event. I simply look at her and say to myself, "And yet I jump higher every day." And soon enough, I'll show them openly that I can indeed fly.

Chapter 5

First Flight

It's the Monday after my suspension and all weekend, up until today, I have made promises after promises to my mother and father that I will not cause any trouble at school. Mainly, I will not debate with the dream killer, Mr. Walker. I agree because I am not too concerned with the naysays of a man who doesn't even make half as much money as a garbage man. Although I'm on my way to school, my mind isn't too concerned with anyone or anything there. I believe I am on the peak of something great and as I go through my day in school and it goes by almost seamlessly because I am calculating and recalculating in my mind the jump I performed that knocked down Mr. David's sign. All weekend, I sat pondering the remarkable feat. Without the proper leverage, a step ladder, or a wall jump, I couldn't have touched it. Come to think of it, on my way to the store during my run, I jumped farther than I had ever jumped and since then, my belly has felt like it is on fire! I can barely concentrate on what I am doing.

My day comes to a screeching halt as I find myself in Mr. Walker's class and as usual, he is going on a rant about how only the privileged are able to make great changes in the world. He goes on to say he himself is the most privileged person he knows and that the only reason he hasn't run for president is that he doesn't want to be in charge of a bunch of idiots. I hate to be a dream killer myself, but I would gladly take a shotgun to his goal because the last thing America needs is a man who thinks that only the rich should prosper. He then turns his attention to Kate and asks her if she still has dreams of being a fashion model with morals. She hesitates and then says "Yes." Walker goes on a rant and raves about how dreamers are so busy with their heads in the clouds that they can't get anything done. He basically told Kate her dream was impossible. He looked at me to see if I would come to her rescue and smirked at me when I sat still and did nothing. Man, this dude aggravates me!

The bell rings and I leave out of the class but wait for Kate to see if she is okay. It's odd; she is usually one of the first people out of the class. As I wait for her, I hear something; it's like a muffled argument and as I put my head closer to the door, I hear footsteps approaching.

I move my head back from the door. Mr. Walker comes walking out with his face as red as a cherry. I look at him and he looks at me and there is dead silence for several seconds. He walks off to the principal's office, probably to complain about one of the few students that he cannot control. Kate walks out after him and her eyes are red like she was just crying and so I ask her if everything all right.

Kate replies, "No, everything is not all right with that man teaching us that we can't do great things. I just had to say something, I was just tired of it!" She looks at me with intensity and then continues, "Thank you for encouraging me and I'm not mad at you for not saying anything today. I know you are probably on thin ice with your parents, which is why he took that shot at you. But he made the mistake of believing that I needed a knight in shining armor to protect me. I can protect myself."

After she was finished talking, I felt kind of embarrassed because I did see myself as a knight that protected the people from the Dragon Walker. Especially the damsel Kate.

I pull my book bag over my shoulder to head to my next class and say, "Well, at least I can take a break from protecting you then, fair lass."

As I move a couple of lockers away she says, "Hey, make sure the break isn't too long, knight." I look back and I can't help but smile at this pretty, strong, intelligent young woman. I walk away with haste so she doesn't see my happiness. After all, my dad did always say, "Leave them wanting more."

The rest of the day goes pretty fast and my stomach is on fire again and I have the urge to run. It's gotten more intense since my run a few days ago and I'm not able to ignore it anymore. When school lets out, I do a quick sprint past the field where my brother practices football to make sure he doesn't want me to stay around. He waves me home and that is where I head. My little sister is hanging out with her friends today, so I have some peace for a couple of hours. I make it home and my parents aren't there—only a note on the refrigerator that says: "Mom and me out for errands. Behave yourself. (That means you JJ.) -Dad."

I don't know why, but reading that note made the fire in my stomach increase to a burning rage. I go up to my room and change into my running clothes and I begin my run. I am not being disobedient, nor am I being disrespectful; my parents haven't said anything about me running or parkour in my spare time, so that's what I am going to do. So I burst out of the door not even bothering to look behind me to see if it is locked. For some reason, I can't be bothered with it right now. I hit the streets with blinding speeds and strong accuracy. I look for the nearest building for wall runs and I see a small store with a fire escape and I take it. I run on the wall to the ladder and climb up but the space of the building isn't so big so I run to the edge and jump off into a role and I continue down the street.

I have been running for at least twelve minutes and I feel more energized with each step. I've reached the leg of my run where all the good parkour spots are and I've noticed this is where I had my first Parkour journey with the PGs. Instead of going into familiar territory, I feel I need to go further than that, so I keep running to find uncharted territory. I find my way toward the old abandoned mill. This was the one place the PGs never took me because all three of them have gotten hurt on a run through this death trap. At least, that's what they called it, but I feel drawn to it. As I try to resist the mill to go somewhere else, I see a flock of birds fly toward the mill. I count it as a coincidence and then I see crows flying toward the mill, and after the crows, several hawks, and after those hawks, I see one little dove fly in the direction of the mill. I have heard eagles will stir the nest of their young in order to get them out of the nest so that they will spread their wings to fly. I think my nest is being stirred; eagles don't know how to fly when they leap from the nest and if they fall too far, the parent will catch them and bring them back to the nest. Only, I don't have parents that can fly — if I fall, and if I fall this time, I might not even survive to heal in a miraculous way.

What do I do? The fire inside me won't rest and it's like it's attracted to the mill. I got it: I will let the cautions and lessons that I have learned over the last few years by my parents. I will let my instincts tell me when to go and when to stop. I'm not that little, inexperienced kid who doesn't know how to hold his own anymore. I'm wiser and more experienced and I know I need to do this. I head for the mill at full speed and I find a gate that is hanging off its edges. I scale it with ease, but I tear my shirt. Okay, make sure I judge the next distance for a jump appropriately. I run inside to the main area and I see a stairway to the roof. That is my goal! I run to the stairs and almost trip. Okay, I need to be aware of my footing so I don't slip. I go up the stairs, across the walkway, and I see there is no way across except for a few chains hanging that I can jump across. I weigh the cost of falling from this height against the thrill of reaching my goal and I jump and almost miss the chains. I use my momentum to swing to the other side of the walkway. Okay, I need to get more momentum to jump across large gaps. I'm almost to the top of the building but the ladder to the roof is rigid. What to do? Okay, use all of my reasoning this time and make a smart choice.

Then it hits me. What did I do at David's Dell? I ran and jumped.

This revelation makes everything so clear to me. This whole time I ran, I didn't make a single mistake until I got to the mill. I'm making mistakes because I'm thinking too much about what I'm doing. Either I can do it or not! Either I have the ability or not! Either I can parkour or not! So what if my friends had a few scrapes and bumps? I am not my friends. I am me and I have yet to have a bump or scrape. I can do this. I can make it to the roof without harm!

I run away from the ladder and I run back to it with swift speed and I lay one foot on the ladder and I jump up the rest of the way to the roof. It was the same sensation I felt in the marketplace—like gravity lost its hold on me and it couldn't hold me down anymore. I can do this, and maybe more. As I land on the roof, I realize what I can and cannot do. And this will be the basis for what I do from this day on. If I say, "I can," then I can, and if I say, "I can't," then I can't.

I see birds at the end of the ledge and they all are looking in my direction. I face them as they all begin to turn around. It's weird but it's like time has slowed down and I see the first thing a bird does before it flies. It jumps and then flaps its wings to soar into the air. I see and understand what to do next, so I start running toward the ledge where there is no other building to hang onto. I reach the ledge and jump into the air and what happens next shocks me but solidifies everything I knew was on the inside of me. I fly!

I am soaring through the air and I can't control it at first, I am actually in the air and I'm not falling to the ground like the last time

I made a foolish jump. This time, I believed beyond what I thought I could believe and look where I am. I am in the place everybody I knew told me I couldn't go, doing what they said I couldn't do. Well, look at me now; all the things I see from this height looks so small, but I can almost focus on cats on the ground. Whoa, is my sight improved? I am up high in the air so I should be lightheaded and dizzy, but I'm not. All this is so wonderful and I don't know how to examine what's going on or where to even start. Maybe I should start at the dream killer's house and ask him if this is possible, but I'm so high in the air, I don't want to come down.

The joy I feel right now is beyond human comprehension, but what I am doing was thought to be beyond human ability too, so I guess a joy I can't explain makes sense right now. I can't seem to stop laughing and crying because I'm doing it. Right now, I have my arms stretched wide like bird wings, I find myself ascending and descending at will. My moments of triumph are dampened a little as I get a call on my cell phone from my sister.

I answer and immediately she says, "Ooh, you're out running, aren't you? I'm gonna tell Momma and Daddy. And what is that in the background it sounds like you got a lot of wind blowing around you?"

The fact that she can hear the sound of wind around me in the air makes me so happy that I am not aggravated by her trying to get me in trouble. I am happy because she can hear it and that means I'm not dead having final thoughts about flying and that I'm not crazy and having a hallucination. I simply reply with laughter, "I will be home faster than you can blink."

I begin to make my way back to the ground but I stop mid-air and say to myself, "You know what? I worked all this time to fly. I should get as much practice in as I can." I slowly begin to ascend into the air, but I fly high enough so no one could see me. I didn't want anyone to see me just yet—after all, I was still processing this myself. There is one thing that concerns me though: as I flew away, I looked back at the mill for memories of my first take off. I saw two shadowy figures watching me, but as I tried to get a better look at them, they disappeared. One had the shape of a woman to the far left of the building and one was the shape of a man to the far right. Maybe I should tell my parents about this event sooner than later because I have a bad feeling about this.

Chapter 6

Documented

The day that I flew was the most wonderful day of my life. I went home after Bella had called me and made it home hours before my mom and dad got home. I was so excited that I could hardly sit still and it was the hardest thing to keep from smiling and to tell the naysayers of my house what I had done. I wanted to tell them in the right way—everything had been tense in my house for the last couple of days because of this rumored miracle, so I held off telling them that day. I had a plan, however. I would wait until tomorrow after school to record myself flying and then show them my actual flight after they saw the video. Foolproof! This way I could see how I did it and show them what I did to the best of my ability.

The next day, after school, I ran home to get my mom's video camera. She had it for two years now and barely used it. Part of the reason she got it was to get me interested in something else other than flying. I have no doubt that if she sees me with it, she will be ecstatic about me using it. I manage to beat everybody home because I was half-flying the entire time, trying not to draw too much attention to myself. I even ran past Kate, barely saying "Hi" because I needed to document what was happening to me. She will be one of the first ones I tell about my new ability.

After I grab the camera, I go to the railroad yard because it barely has any people around, especially on the weekday. After I saw those two figures at the mill, I don't feel comfortable going back there. I hope they didn't see my face, but even if they did, they wouldn't know who I was. Then again, I can only hope they don't know who I am.

I set up the camera on a tripod and begin my documentary with a little warm-up exercise to stay limber and stretched out. I begin with by saying, "Okay, this is flying doc one. I have recently learned I have the ability to fly and I'm making this documentary to show that one, I am not crazy and two, I need everyone in the world to know dreams come true if you seek after them. And for all of you who said I couldn't do it, boom! In your face, I proved you wrong! Being serious now, it seems to be connected with just being able to believe I was able to, even though everyone told me I couldn't. Now, mind you, I did everything to fly ranging from parkour to gymnastics and every other thing in between. These things helped me physically, but not flight-wise. If it could, I think everybody would be able to fly—unless we are able to just do something uniquely different. At this point, I'm willing to believe that because I can fly, so why can't other miraculous things be possible? Now, I jumped higher and farther than I ever jumped a couple of days ago when my sister made me mad and I was able to knock down a high sign. Yesterday, however, I left the ground in flight and didn't land until I got home. So we are going to see how this works, okay? So let's start with this: hovering."

I walk a few paces back from the camera so it can catch all my actions. I bend my knees and I lift off the ground about one meter into the air and I hover, almost throwing myself off balance. I come back down to the ground and start laughing. I look into the camera and say "Whoa, okay, that is sustained flight for all of you who are skeptical. I repeat: sustained flight." I look down and launch several meters into the air and hover back and forth trying to stay in the frame of the camera. I land and start laughing again because I know that I am not crazy and I have proof for anyone who would doubt me.

I realize it is time to take it to the next level, so I grab the camera and say, "Okay, it is established that I can fly, so let's see how fast, high, and far I can fly." I blast off into the air at high speeds with enough force to move the small crates that were around me. In seconds I'm above the clouds and I see nothing but a sea of blue sky and I begin to explore the open air. Now I can see from the exhilarating feeling going through my body why birds like flying so much. I used to be jealous of them, but not now! There is no need to be jealous; I can fly myself and I'm glad I don't have to covet what I have. There are a lot of cumulous clouds today, which usually means it is going to rain, but that's not a problem for me. Now, I can just fly over the clouds to stay dry. Even if I got wet, I would be able to air dry within minutes.

The camera is still rolling and I'm letting it catch all the sights and sounds that I know are impossible for me to get off the internet. I also let it catch some of the expressions on my face before I go back to documenting while I am in the air. I look into the camera and say, "Okay, so here I am, in the clear blue sky and I am not lightheaded. I say that because I know the higher you go into the sky, the thinner the air gets, and I'm pretty high. It seems my body is automatically compensating for what I am able to do right now. A scientist might call this a form of microevolution, which is a smart way to say adaptation. Even now, I'm looking down from where I am and my eyesight seems to have binocular vision. I can see clearer and farther than I used to. Even while I was in school today, I noticed a spider on Kate's shoulder that I would have normally had to focus on to find, but I picked it out without even trying. My breathing is not labored at all and I feel like I can take in a month's worth of air.

"I can't begin to understand how to explain all of this, after all, I'm not a scientist, but I guess the simplest of all explanations is that when you believe in something hard enough, the rest of you has no choice but to follow. Your body will change to suit what you are constantly thinking, what you are constantly believing. I believed I could fly, so I did everything in my power to bring it out so I guess karate, boxing, gymnastics, parkour, and all the other crazy stuff I've done just help reinforce what I believed and bring out what I knew was there. You can't let anyone else dictate what you can or cannot do. Not too sound prolific, but hey, maybe a great sage is for me too. I probably should take some philosophy classes or something. I don't know; I'll deal with that later, but now it's time for more flying."

I take off into the air, not even caring about the video that I'm making. Right now, I'm just going to enjoy the wind in my face while my back is to every doubt I myself may have ever had. Trust and believe I have had them, but through it all, I've learned to have faith and press through until it came to pass and now it's time to share my dream with everybody else. I'm not selfish; I want to share this moment with my family even though they told me I couldn't. Maybe they think these types of things are impossible because they just haven't seen them done. Well, it's time to show them and I'm headed home to do it right now.

But as I get ready to fly home, I look down onto a building and see the shadowy figure again. This time I blast down to see who this is because I don't believe too heavily in coincidence and whoever this person is knows I can fly and I have a feeling I know who this is. As I approach the building where I see the figure, she is standing in the door that leads down into the building so her face is shadowed, and even with my new vision I can't seem to get a good fix on her but when she speaks it's no doubt who she is.

She speaks to me in a mellow voice and says, "Well it looks like you kept on believing even after all this time. I was sure your father would have talked some sense into you."

I reply with, "What do you mean, 'talk some sense into' me? What did he know? That this would happen or something?"

May speaks to me in the sweetest voice ever, trying to calm me down. "Listen to me, Jason. All will be explained in due time, but I think that it would be best if you got rid of that tape for your safety and the safety of your family. There's a world that you don't know about. Now that you can fly, you will attract a lot of unwanted attention and this tape will just add to the hassle. I will even say your family doesn't need to know just yet either."

I reply in anger, "Wait! For what? Listen, lady, I'm not even sure who you are, but if you haven't noticed, my family and friends think I'm a nut and my flying and this tape in my hand will show them otherwise. I'm not listening to you—especially when you come off at me sounding all cryptic!"

Nurse May looks at me and laughs before answering, "Wow, you are just like your father. When he was your age, he had a short temper just like you have right now. The passion I see in your eyes are the same I saw in his too. Okay, listen: I will let you think on this for a little while but know I don't think you should go home right now. Something bad is waiting for you and your family doesn't even realize the trouble they may have put themselves in."

With great alarm, I ask her what she means and how she knows my dad so well, but she refuses to answer and goes into the doorway that leads to the building. I rush behind her to get answers, but when I open the door, she is gone without a trace. I know there is no way she can get down all the stairs without me seeing her, but she is really gone.

I look around in a state of confusion wondering how an excellent day could have turned on me so fast. She told me not to go home right now, but if my family is in danger I have to go—especially if it is because of my doing. I blast off into flight in the direction of my home and I'm worried about what I will find when I get there. Maybe there is scientist out there who knows what I can do or maybe my dad has some deep dark secret that put us all in danger and I just opened Pandora's box by accident. No, I'm not going to assume. I'm just going to go home and hope for the best. I'm an optimist, remember? I can't start expecting the bad now because some lady from my past said something might happen. Maybe she's a head case and I just said what I said while I'm on my way home by flight! Gotta get home, now!

Chapter 7

Psychiatrists!?

As I hurry home, a million thoughts race through my head about everything that has gone on. Not so much about how I can fly, but about how May talked about my dad. From the way she spoke, it was like they had some kind of history together and what is scarier is she made it sound like he knew I would be able to unlock this ability if I kept trying. If that is the case and she knows my dad, then my father has some explaining to do because I can see nothing wrong coming from a person having the ability to fly. The trip home doesn't take long, but I'm alarmed to see a black car sitting in front of my house as I approach. The car looks like a 2015 Lexus with tinted windows, so whoever is in my house looks like they have a lot of cash. Instead of going through the front door,

I silently fly over to the side of my house to take a look through the window.

I look through and see my mother in tears and my father consoling her. Bella is not in the house; I think I saw her going in the direction of the marketplace with some of her friends. There is a man sitting across from my parents in a chair with his leg folded over the other and his hand on his chin, almost like the thinker. No one notices me as I spy through the glass and hear them speak.

The man on the other side of the room starts with: "Mrs. Jackson, I can assure you that your husband contacting me was just out of pure concern for your son. From what I hear, this can just be an overactive imagination that we are dealing with. There is no need to work yourself up; we will just take Jason to my office and sit down and talk about these dreams that he has been having. We will not put him in a straightjacket."

He laughs, but from the way this man talks, he sounds like he could be a politician and I would almost believe him about not putting me in a straightjacket if it were not for the two goons I see standing on each side of him. Both of them look like bodybuilders and they probably know how to hold their own in a fight. No doubt Dad told them about my fighting skills.

I hover up to my room window, but I pass my brother's room on the way. Jackie is in his room sitting on his bed with his fist bald up like he is ready to fight. No doubt he's seen the people downstairs. I know my brother, so I already know what's in his head; he will fight them both if they try to take me by force, but I don't want him getting hurt. Both of those men look like professional fighters and the man in the chair looks fit too. I will not be selfish and get anybody hurt, but I do know what I will do! As I hover to my room window and open it quietly so no one will hear me, I creep over to my desk and I grab a pencil and paper to write a note. It reads: "Dear Family, Since you apparently think I am crazy, I can prove to you that I know how to fly. On this DVD is recorded evidence of what I am able to do. Look at it and see it for yourself. -JJ the Dreamer."

I figure someone will eventually come into my room and look around to miss me if I'm not home by tomorrow morning. So I will leave this note in my room with the DVD so they will come and get me out if I'm in an asylum somewhere, but I plan to show this mystery guy what I can do myself if he makes the wrong diagnosis. The only downside I see is if they see I can actually fly, I might end up on a table being experimented on so the world will know how

I tick. I'm damned if I do and damned if I don't, but at least they will all know the truth about me and the impossible.

I've decided to make a copy of the DVD on my computer just in case something happens to the original. My computer was already on, so I'm not making a lot of noise burning a copy. I'm leaving this copy for my brother because right now if everyone else fails the one who looks up to me will be on my side. We learned pig Latin when we were little to get secrets around my sister, so I wrote a note and put it down on the desk so he won't have to look too far to get to the evidence. It reads: "Dear AckieJay, Ooklay on the iscday! I ancay yfly."

One day, we were bored and got tired of Bella telling on us when we went to sneak cookies before dinner, so we learned a new language. It basically says: "Dear Jackie, Look on the disc! I can fly."

I sneak back out of my window and I fly a few blocks away so I can walk home. When I get to the front of the door, I pretend like I don't know what is going on and as I go into the house I ask, "What is the problem?"

My dad asks me to come and sit by him in a solemn tone. He continues with, "Son, this is a friend of mine. He is Doctor Belial and he is a psychiatrist. I wanted him to talk to you about what has happened the last few days."

I respond with, "The last few days? What about them? I got into a fight with a bully, I got suspended, and I was grounded the whole time I was here."

Doctor Belial interrupts, "Yes, but I'm more interested in what the fight was about and how I can help prevent similar events from happening again in the future."

This is the reason I don't like these type of doctors. Yes, some things are deep-rooted and deep-seated, but other things are not. I got into a fight with a chump who thought he could pick on me about my dream of flying. Of course, I know everyone here wants to talk about the elephant in the room they are too afraid to so I play along.

"Will I have to go somewhere with you, Mr. Doctor?"

He smiles and answers, "Yes, son. I think that would be best so as to not further upset your mother."

Oh, he just played the mother card. I don't like this guy too much. I ask him how long will we be gone and he answers with a sinister smile, "Just for the next couple of hours."

I'm not anxious about going with this guy, especially after that smile, but I see the men standing next to him tense up a little. Trust me: when you know how to fight, you can sense these type of things in others. I feel my father nudge me and so I look at him and he nods. I don't want to go because something about this feels all wrong and I just want to hover in the air right now to show everybody flight is possible. Yet, I can't I feel like I'm in danger—as a matter of fact, I've felt it since I walked through the door and this guy seems kind of familiar. For some reason, I think flight right now would do more harm than good. If something turned south, then me, Dad, and Jackie could defend ourselves, but I don't know if Momma could. Although she is a pest, Bella could walk through that door at any minute. I haven't the time to sit here and ponder all the possible scenarios, so I decided to go with him.

I look back at my mom and dad as I leave the house with Dr. Belial and I'm waiting for them to stop them and tell me that I can come back into the house now. They don't. As I get into the car, I can see my brother come to the porch as I look at the reflection on the glass window. I get in and it's like I stepped into a dark world that is accompanied by a harsh and intense feeling of dread. As we drive down the road, I can see my sister returning home with her friends looking into the car to see who is driving. We pass her quickly and we head down the road toward Oak and Ave Streets, which is about a twenty-minute drive and an hour walk. It's about a thirty-minute run though—trust me, I know.

We turn a couple of corners until we stop in front of this big red building that has no name on it. We go inside to the first floor and I'm led to Dr. Belial's office space alone. His office is small with several cabinets on each side, filled with psychology books and a couple of anatomy books. He sits behind his oak wood desk in a red leather chair and I sit on the other side into a wooden chair with a soft padded bottom.

We stare at each other for several minutes. I think he wants to ask me about why I think I will one day be able to fly and, well, I don't know what else he is thinking and staring at this dude for so long I get the sense that I don't want to know. He has an eerie feeling about him that makes me not want to relax. I've been plotting my escape since I got in the car and since I can fly now, it wouldn't be too hard to get out of the window and soar straight to my house.

He snickers a little and says to me, "Well JJ. Oh, do you mind if I call you JJ? I have heard a lot about you from your dad and he is quite concerned about your mental well-being."

I say, "Is that so."

He replies with, "Yes, he is, and with good reason. For some reason, you think you can fly. You're a fifteen-year-old boy who should be more concerned with girls, sports, and test-taking. Now, for a child to have this dream is fine because children will be children and they will grow out of it as time passes. But you, you hold on to this dream even though physics, chemistry, biology, and every other known scientific law say that you can't. Why?"

I respond to his smug response with confidence because he has yet to see the blue sky the way I've just seen it. "Well, that is a simple answer, doctor. I believe in everyday miracles. The miracle of flying in a metal container with several turbines tied to its wings. The miraculous ability of a doctor to go into a man's head and cut out a tumor while the patient loses only a teaspoon of blood. Oh, and what about the countless traumatic events in a person's life that should have driven them insane but they are right as rain helping others? That is a miracle. So seeing all that, why shouldn't I believe I could fly one day?"

Doctor Belial smiles at me and says, "My dear boy, what you are talking about is science. Science can achieve anything and—"

I interrupt him rudely, "And science has said one thousand years ago flight was impossible. Science once said removing a tumor without cutting into the man's head was impossible! Science is nothing but knowledge it changes as we accumulate more of it, so I don't care about man's current ignorance of human flight or any other ability we as a species may have. Because I believe we are in living in a time when we won't be held in the dark about such matters anymore. And I know I am one of the people in the world that's meant to show this to be true."

Belial loses his smile and says, "You think you are?"

"No. I know I am."

There is dead silence for at least several minutes as he looks into my eyes and I look back at his, wondering why he seems so familiar. He breaks the silence and says, "Unless you give me proof, I won't believe the dream of a child."

That upsets something fierce in me, because without thinking, I lifted into the air, hovering over his desk to make sure he knew this was no hoax. I stay in the air looking at him with his jaw dropped low and I say, "Is this enough proof?"

He begins to laugh and slowly gets up from his chair in a calm manner. I'm a bit uneasy because it's not every day that you see a man defy the laws of physics and he is shrugging off this scientific groundbreaking event like it is nothing.

He walks calmly around the desk to the door and locks it. I'm definitely on guard now because that makes me think that he doesn't want me to leave. And now I feel odd and my vision is getting blurry. My body feels heavy and I feel myself descending onto the desk and then I fall sloppily to the floor. He didn't stick me with anything, so I don't know what's going and now I see green smoke begin to feel the room. It's making my throat scratchy and my eyes watery.

I hear the doctor say, "My dear boy, do not worry. This is a special type of sedative meant for special people like you so you won't die. And if you are wondering why I'm not in shock and awe, it is simply because I deal with special people on a regular basis and although I've never encountered one who could fly, I've already seen you do it."

Now how could he have seen me fly no one was around when I took off into the air. No one except—those two dark figures! One was Nurse May the other was this guy. I look at him in shock and in pain as he walks to me and kneels, saying, "Aw, he remember me now. Don't worry, young one. I have plans for you, big plans. The *dark* is in need of you."

I pass out and everything fades to black.

Chapter 8

More Than You Know

The last thing I saw was some ugly dude's face telling me that I was important and I was needed by—I don't know—the *dark* or something. I feel like I'm tied down to a table or something and I can't move my arms or legs. I hear this low humming, like the sound a light bulb makes. I think whatever that crazy doctor hit me with is wearing off. As a matter of fact, I'm starting to see straight again. I'm looking straight up and there is a ceiling lamp over my face. The thing is so bright it feels like it's going to burn a hole through my head. A shadowed figure's head hovers over me and all I can see is the silhouette, but when I hear him say "hello," I know it's Doctor Belial.

He asks me how I'm doing, as if he didn't know that I'm scared, mad, and angry for being strapped down like some animal. I try to struggle but it's no use. I can't break free, let alone fly. Well, I haven't tried yet, but I don't want to try just so Dr. Jekyll here can put me back to sleep. He tries to calm me down by rubbing my forehead but that just makes me mad and I start struggling all over again. A man doesn't rub another man's forehead—especially when he can't move!

He gets my attention with little a vapor of green mist hovering over my face. He asks if I would like to know how he does this and goes on a rant. He begins with, "I'm not sure how I do this. I know this little vapor holds several chemicals that are sedatives. I know there is a chemical used for inducing tears in the eye ducts. I know it weakens the body and can cause a blackout for days, minutes, and in your case, one hour. Truthfully, no chemical mixture of this caliber should be able to be sustained like it is, let alone over your face without being inhaled by either one of us, but here it is. Young man, I don't know how I am able to do this, just like you don't fully understand how you are able to fly, but what I do know is we can do what we do because we believe we can."

He causes the vapor to disappear and walks to the left side of the table and continues talking. "When I was little, I was fascinated with chemistry. I couldn't get enough of it. How we are able to mix different compounds and always get different results. We are able to cure cancer, malaria, even AIDs if we wanted to with just a little ingenuity, effort, and understanding of the periodic table. But at the age of seventeen, I found I wasn't happy with the norm of the once glorious process. I found I wanted more, I wanted to do more! I started believing that this wasn't it. I started believing I could affect molecules a lot more than what I was doing. I found myself believing I could master the chemicals in these beakers and test tubes and one day, I found that they obeyed my will.

"I was in school and I had reached a dead-end with one of my experiments and I almost gave up. That is, until my former girl-friend, Myra, walked in on me as I threw a glass beaker across the room filled with a dangerous chemical. It splashed on her and she fell to the ground convulsing, twitching and screaming. I rushed over to her and found myself helpless. I couldn't even stop her agony until I said, 'Yes, I can.' I began wiping the chemicals away, but they floated off with the wave of my hands. Each drop turned into vapor and I was able to direct it where I wanted it to go. I was even able to pull the chemicals out of her body that seeped through the pores of her skin.

"I learned how to do the impossible and probably, like your body has, my body made the proper adaptations. After that day, chemistry came so much easier to me and there was no problem within this field that I could not solve. If I haven't made a miracle cure, it's only because my personal being has no need of it yet. I was even able to fix the damage that was caused by the chemical bath my young love had to endure and for a time, she was grateful and even more enamored with me for my new abilities. I learned, as all young men do, abilities will only get you so far in the eyes of a woman.

"She left me for the high school jock who only had the ability to run a few yards and throw a piece of pigskin. She left me, *ha ha*! She left me for someone who hadn't even had a fully evolved brain yet. My love told me that it wasn't his muscles that she saw, but it was his heart. So I started thinking, what if his heart was as dark as the dreaded night? I formed a concoction and in the same way I drugged you, I drugged him and caused a mental impairment that causes him to lash out at anyone in anger. The first was his mother, then his father, his teachers, and friends, and last but not least, my love. But the one that made my day happy was the off-duty cop who had to shoot him in order to protect his own life.

"Surely my love would come running back to me and I again would feel the warm embrace of her arms. Myra came to my home and as I opened the door she rushed in, I thought to kiss me, but it was to smack me in my face. She said to me, 'I know it was you who hurt Derek and I will tell everyone what you can do and everyone will know you for the monster you are!' She stormed out on me, and again my heart was broken. Not only had I lost her for sure, but she would tell everyone of my newfound ability—who knows what would have happened to me. That is, if she told the tale.

"I went to her house late that night when everyone was sleeping and I crept in through her bedroom window. She was a hard sleeper, so she didn't hear me come in. I had thought to make a chemical that would keep her, silent but her voice was so sweet, it would have been a sin against nature to silence her in such a way. But then I realized the chemical I needed was already in her room: the chemicals in her brain. This was new to me but so was this new level of mastery over chemicals, and so I thought all the brain needs to function is the right chemicals in the right place at the right time.

"I could cause memory cells to die or maybe even cause blood clots—who knew what those possibilities were at the time. They were endless."

About this time I am extremely horrified not only at this dude's terribly long tale, but also at the fact that someone who is as twisted as this can have the ability to believe and awaken an extraordinary skill. His face now turns sad as he finishes his tale.

"I was, however, immature at that skill. I hadn't tested it, so when I began to manipulate the chemicals in her mind, I gave her horrible nightmares and then horrible pain. One cannot bend another without causing some kind of discomfort. She began yelling louder and louder until she woke her parents and those fools came rushing in.

"Her father tried to run to me, but I had poison in my pocket and so I sent it down his throat and her mother's, only to incapacitate them. I had enough mastery over the chemical to cause only the pain I saw was necessary. I went back to work on Myra and the more I twisted and turned her, the more I sought aid from the solutions I had been carrying, just in case I would fail. I sent every chemical I had into her body to try to remake her mind, but sadly I failed and killed her instead. Her parents could barely say a word as I stood over Myra's lifeless body, but they did manage to say, 'Please help.' So I did. I let the poison do its work and I sent them off to be with my beloved Myra.

"Of course, later, with more experimentation, I found that no person can be manipulated without external drugs of some kind. So don't worry about dying when I open your mind to new possibilities."

I respond to this madman with, "What are you talking about?! You are a murderer and my parents will know something is up when I walk in all boozed up, jerk! Now let me go right now!"

Doctor Belial begins talking again as he walks toward me with a needle filled with green fluid. "Aw, my boy, you mean your parents who called me in the first place to help you with your imaginary goal of flying? It's funny, your father called me in as a favor I owed him from our younger days. He might not have called me if he knew what you know. Some skeletons need to be kept in the closet. But don't worry about them. I sent my one of my friends to take care of them."

I'm shocked, speechless, as I ask what he means.

As he injects me with the chemicals which burn like crazy, he tells me, "My boy, the two men who were with me are just like you. Only, they are stronger but not as smart after I had my go at their minds. I sent one of them to take care of your family so you could leave that life behind and embark on a brand new adventure. The world is bigger than you know and I must make sure you walk the right path when you awake from this mundane existence into a marvelous life."

He puts his forehead to mine and all of a sudden, whatever he injected me with starts burning throughout my body, especially in my head.

I can feel him messing with whatever is on the inside of my mind and it's painful! It's strange, but I can feel his voice talking to me and it like he is trying to rewrite me. It feels like he is trying to make his thoughts my own. Dr. Jekyll puts a new twist on the term "brainwashing" because that is what I feel like he is doing. As a matter of fact, I'm sure of it. He is trying to brainwash me. All I can do is scream! *Ahhhh!* I hear him talking to me over and over again saying "Break, break, break, break." And I feel obliged to do it just to end the pain. No! I didn't let a fall break me and I was racked with all kinds of pain and it felt a lot worse than this. I'm not about to let some weirdo with a crummy mustache and beard do what falling couldn't do with half as much pain.

I'm going to fight back and I'm going to win. I didn't break when the dream killer took a shot at me. I'm not going to break for somebody who doesn't even know my struggle. Someone who doesn't know what I've been through to get where I am! One of the reasons I wanted to fly was for free so I could escape gravity and all the negativity it holds and I refuse to be anybody's caged bird! So I say *get off!*

At that moment, some kind of energy burst out of me in the commotion, knocking the doctor away and breaking the bonds that held me. I get off the table with haste and find my way to the door. I look back at the doctor and he looks at me, shocked at what just happen. He wastes no time in sending more of his funky mist my way and I waste no time in flying up the stairs. Apparently, he dragged me into the basement of the building when I was out. There is nobody in the lobby so I don't act shy with flying right now, not sure I would, even if someone was around because there is madman out to get me. I fly toward the exit and I see the shadow of one of the men who came in with us earlier, standing in the next room. The doctor said he was stronger than me so I can't risk him getting a hold of me even while flying.

There is a desk nearby so I crouch down behind it and there is a fire hydrant next to me. This gives me an idea, but before I can work out the bugs, Doctor Belial comes out of the basement screaming, "Get him, you fool!"

The goon comes rushing out of the other room and Doctor Belial shoots a cloud of green vapor rushing in my direction; it's now or never! I fly toward the exit with the hydrant, I get past the goon, making my way out of the door, but he grabs my leg. Man, the doctor wasn't kidding. This dude is strong. Well, that's why I have plan B. I take the hydrant and spray it in his face and then I smash the base of it against his forehead while flying in his direction. He gets knocked down, causing him to loosen his grip, but it's enough that I can get away, even if he did tear my favorite workout pants.

I get out of the door just before I breathe in any of that mist that almost surrounds me. I waste no time getting up high into the air outside of Doctor Belial's reach. He may be able to do something impossible like me, but he sure can't fly. I race to home to tell my family about what happened, still feeling the effects of that drug inside of me. I decide to land and run home so I can sweat it out and it works. My sweat is green and the more I sweat, the better I feel. I'm not too worried about Belial driving up in his car to catch me because I still can parkour. Trust me, I may be able to fly, but I didn't spend all those years learning Parkour so I could lose it.

I run to my house and I'm horrified to see one of the men coming out of my home and getting into a white van, pulling off. I couldn't let him see me, so I wait for him to turn the corner before I sprint to my home. I walk in, horrified at the scene, all the furniture is broken almost like it was made to look vandalized. I hear moaning in the kitchen and to my surprise, it's my dad. He looks beat up, but not too bad. I look for my brother, sister, and mother and find they are not in the house. I start to panic because I remember that crazy man said he would kill them so I wouldn't have a life to turn back to. I get a call on my cell and the caller ID says, "Momma."

I pick up with haste and say, "Momma, Momma, are you okay?"

Then a chilling voice says "She fine for now. I stopped my friend from completing his work just before he finished your father. He sure is spry for a man his age."

I demand the whereabouts of my family and Belial just says, "The place where you first took flight" and he hangs up.

I have no idea what to do, who knew learning about something so great could lead to so much danger. But I can't stay here and I won't let him kill my family either. It's selfish of him to take them away and it would be selfish to let them suffer for me.

Chapter 9

Something's Not Right

Before I fly off to the mill to save my family, I help my dad to the couch. He is pretty banged up, but not too bad. It's funny, I could barely get away from goon two. I don't know how my dad managed to hold his own against goon one for however much amount of time he did. I was sure goon one would have made short work of him. I guess I should stop making fun of him behind his back about being old. Whatever he did bought the rest of my family enough time so by the time that I escaped, Belial had to make the call to stop the murder and mayhem. I don't know if that is a good thing or bad thing. Belial probably made his thug stop so he could take my family as hostages to get me to come to him. Unfortunately, that plan is about to work.

As I head out, I lock the door behind me and I make sure no one else is around before I take off into the air. I thought about calling the police, but what was I going to tell them? "Hey a man who can control poison and two mini goliaths just beat up my dad and kidnapped my family. Oh and that's not all—they are doing this because I just found out that I can fly so it's kinda my fault." They would hang up the phone on me so fast it wouldn't have been funny. Plus, even if they did come, how can they fight someone like this who has committed murder and basically gotten away with it? The cops would be slaughtered before they could pull their guns and look at me talking. I can only fly! What am I supposed to do? Fly them into a tree and hope the fire department doesn't come get them down?

No, I have to focus. If I'm going to get my family to safety and get out of this alive, I have to work smarter, not harder. The bodyguards are stronger than me and might be just as fast as me, judging from how quick the one guy grabbed me, but they can be hurt. So I'm going for the eyes and sensitive areas on their bodies, but Belial is the real problem. I don't want to get too close to him and have him take me out with some type of sedative. I'm stumped. I've learned how to punch bigger guys in boxing, I've learned how to throw fat guys in karate, and I've learned how to get around guys without wasting too much energy in parkour, but this? I guess I will have to play it by ear and when all else fails, then I guess I will believe I can beat them. No, there is no guessing about it. I believe I can beat them!

I'm just now getting to the mill and I see them parked just inside the gate. The gate looks like it's been bent from both sides and tossed to the ground like it was paper. No doubt this was done to show me what I'm up against so I would just give up. I see my family in the van using my heightened vision and I am relieved to see they are okay, but I can't focus too much on them. Belial and his buddies are standing in front of the van looking right at me. I descend several meters away from them but I don't land on the ground. I want to keep as much leverage on them as I can. I size all three of them up to see how to best handle them, but one thing I can't do is lose my temper. I keep losing my temper and I keep getting into trouble because of it. I have to stay calm. Like my old sensei used to say, "It is all right to be angry; there are some things a person needs to be angry about, but don't let it cloud your judgment. Focus and seek to solve the problem without blind rage."

As I am thinking about how to solve this problem, Belial calls out to me, "Young man! I know you are thinking about how to save your family and beat us. But you must know that at the end of this ordeal, they must still die and you must come to me."

I answer back, "If they must still die, then why are they living now?"

Belial smirks at me and says, "Simple. Live bait catches more fish."

I beg and plead with him to let them go but he shakes his head. I even offer to just give myself up in exchange for them just to buy some time, but what he says next not only scares me, but shows me that you can never negotiate with a devil.

He says, "No, my boy. I must have your undivided attention. They would only serve as a distraction. You don't seem to under-stand there is a power in you that you don't even comprehend yet. I have felt it and when I turn you over to the *dark,* we will not simply be its agents, but we will come to rule it as headmasters."

I have no idea what this guy is talking about, but it all sounds so bad and wrong. Before I even know it, he sends a cloud of vapor over to the van so he can suffocate my family. I shout *"Nooooo!"* and fly in my enemy's direction.

The two goons are first in my way. The one on the left that I call goon one rushes toward me and jumps high into the air, about the same distance I jumped when I knocked David's sign down.

He tries to come down on me, but I swerve out of the way and he misses. Goon two comes and throws a wild haymaker at me, but I fly low and avoid the punch. I try to head for Belial, but goon two grabs my left leg and pulls me back into a fight with him. I can feel myself being yanked through the air and slammed violently on the ground. This guy is no joke; it feels like I've been hit by a bus. He steps into my stomach, causing me to gag a little and then kicks me in the direction of goon one. Goon one picks me up and bear hugs me to the point that I can't breathe. I can tell if he wanted to break me in half, he could, but he won't. I think his master wants me alive without too much damage.

As I rest in the arms of this man's tight grip I look back to see that the cloud has reached the van and is slowly seeping into it. I can hear my sister and brother begin to choke although they are unconscious. My mom is in the far back and the gas has just reached her but instead of choking, she lets out a painful gasp. That's it! No one puts their hands on my mother! But I can't get mad and lose control again. I have to focus and get away from this guy who is breaking my back. Wait—he hasn't broken my back. He's only trying to make me pass out. That's their flaw. They are subject to Belial and he wants me on his side so he won't let them do irreversible damage to me. And now I see that I'm in a position to poke this guy in the eye!

With all my strength, I poke him in the eyes and plug my fingers in his nose and he shouts, loosening his grip on me. It's all I need to get into the air while he is holding me. As we go up higher and higher, I can tell this guy doesn't like heights. I threaten to fall if he doesn't let me go and he lets go on his own and falls to the ground. Man, Belial didn't foresee when he brainwashes a person, they sometimes loose basic common sense.

I recompose myself for a second and go after goon two. I don't make the mistake of underestimating his speed again. I fly around, kicking him and punching him in his throat, shins, groin, and eyes to get him off balance. When he is disoriented enough, I go for his chest and sides throwing nothing but body shots. I stay there too long and he hammers me to the ground but I quickly recoil and go for his legs, lifting off into the air holding him by his ankles. Man, is this dude heavy.

As I continue my ascent, I notice goon one has recovered and has jumped into the air to grab me again. I let go of goon two and they collide, but I quickly grab onto goon two's legs again and take them both high into the air. I head over in the direction of the mill, right in the center of the building, and I give both of them a childish look like they know what I'm about to do. They both look at me and start shaking their heads back and forth, but I nod my head up and down and I let them go. I figure since they are so strong, the fall won't kill them and that when they get back up, it will be at least a couple of hours. The sound these two makes is like a bowling ball crashing into a wall. I don't know who to feel sorrier for: them or the mill.

I turn my attention to Belial, rushing to him with all my speed, but just before I get to him, a large cloud of vapor surrounds him. I can't get too close to him because even from this distance, the effects of the gas are felt. I can hear him snickering and laughing as the cloud grows bigger. I don't know what to do. I can't pound on him with all this poison around—and speaking of poison, I don't think my family can last much longer. I look over at them and they are still coughing and gagging. I have to think of something.

Belial begins to taunt me "You honestly think you can beat me, Peter Pan? You must be joking!"

Did this dude really just call me "Peter Pan"? Oh yeah, I'm pounding him into the dust now. Belial sends the vapor after me and I fly in the direction of the mill. I look back and I notice the vapor in the car is seeping out as well. Whoa! I didn't think of this before, but maybe this guy has limits. He even expressed his limits about how he can't control someone without the aid of a drug. He must not be able to multitask with such a great cloud of vapor and his focus on me. I have a plan now and it's called "tag."

As Belial sends the cloud toward me, I lead it into the sky and then I rush back down, side-swiping Belial on his left side. The vapor rushes down to his aid and I quickly evacuate the area, retreating back into the sky. The vapor follows as planned and I go back down to pay Belial a little visit again. This time, with a sweeping back kick that knocks him to the ground. I fly in the direction of the mill and I begin to beat the psychiatrist at his own mind games.

"Hey Doctor B, I can see why Myra left you for that jock! All this power and you can't catch little old Peter Pan. All brain and no bronze makes for a dull time, don't you agree?"

He looks at me with evil and anger in his eyes and chases me into the mill. He shouts at me, "You insolent little rat! I was going to leave some of your mind when I awoke you unlike my body-guards, but now I will make it so that you will not have the thinking capacity of a roach when I am through with you!"

Okay, I guess I hit a nerve with that last comment, but at least he is away from my family. Now I have to keep his attention on me. I answer his call, "Yeah right, just like Myra's mind. Remind me, whatever happened to her mind, again? Oh yeah, an inexperienced novice got in her head and killed her!"

All of a sudden the cloud vapor thickens and comes at me with great speed.

I fly through the doors of the mill followed by the vapor clouds bursting through the windows. It is congested in here and there is no free-flowing air. I have to get out of here. I guess the doc knows what I'm thinking, so he sends vapor clouds toward the only exit in the roof where the rigid stairs are. Man, what am I going to do? Wait—I remember toward the center of the mill is where the goons fell and left a big hole in the ceiling, I have to get to there, now! I fly at great speeds, but it is so crowded in here that I can't fly like I want to, but I won't let that stop me. I know how to parkour the fastest way between any two points. As I run, with a combination of flying, I can feel the vapor narrowly grabbing me as I jump over benches and swing around poles. I maneuver to different levels of the factory, using wall runs and explosive high jumps combined with flying.

I can see my exit is within sight and I can see the vapor converging on that point so I have to hurry. But in the distance, I can see two shadows running at me, screaming. Oh no, it's goon one and goon two. Not even a fall from seven stories or more could kill them! At least I won't be charged with murder or attempted murder.

I just wanted to knock them out, and apparently, I failed at that too!

I use this as an opportunity to get some speed and leverage. I run

straight for them and jump to run on their heads. I kick a barrel

of dirt into their eyes to blind them so they won't catch me. This

time, I can't afford to let that happen right now. As they are dis-

oriented, I succeed in the head run and I blast off into the hole of

the ceiling, leaving the goons in the factory to be choked by the

poison pursuing me.

I barely make it through, going high into the sky to escape

the mist that surrounded me, gaging and coughing, hoping for a

moment's reprieve. I'm shocked, however, to see Belial looking at

me from on the roof of the mill. He looks at me smiling, not saying

a thing like he knows he has me beat.

He then speaks to me and says, "I congratulate you! You

manage to get me away from your family and the poison I sent has

probably lost some effect. You got me to focus on you with your

little jabs at me about my former love that I had all but forgotten

about my bait I have in the car. I most likely killed my two body-

guards as well with this massive attack. But the poison inhaled by

your family has done enough damage that when they don't receive

medical help, they will die. However, I don't want to kill you and you can't beat me. So why don't you just come down here and we will finish what I started in my lab. Or I will send my vapor up there to get you. You are tired and exhausted; there isn't too much more even you can do."

He then holds up a needle and syringe with more of that green chemical in it and motions for me to come to him.

Man, talk about arrogance, but he is right. I am tired and this vapor is everywhere. I have to do something, though. What I need is a strong wind or a tornado—and then it clicks. Tornadoes are caused by air moving in a circular motion. Hot and cold air chase each other around and that is followed by an upward draft which creates suction. Or a fan moving at high speeds will blow air—I just have to fly around fast in order to do it. Can I do it? That is a little much, even for me. Yet, look at where I am. I am in the sky, flying. Why should I stop pushing the boundaries now and why should I let some demented fool tell me what my boundaries are? I just need to believe and my body and the power I have will do the rest. I just need to believe.

I'm doing it!

Chapter 10

I'm Just Like you

I motion for Belial to send his gas up to get me. He frowns at me and sends up the vapor that filled the mill. I have no idea how he created all this poison, but in order for this plan to work, I need for all his gas to come at me so I can disarm him completely. As the cloud amasses and grows larger and larger, I sit in the sky waiting for my chance to take off and see if I can pull off this insane plan. The fire in my stomach starts to burn again like the time I first jumped high and the first time I took flight into the skies. I come back to this simple thought: *Either I can do it or not.* I know I can do this.

Then, right when the vapor clouds look like a dragon ready to consume me, I take off in a burst of speed around the cloud, going in circles, just out of its reach. I make sure to circle from top to bottom so I can encompass the giant mass. I go faster and faster each pass around, pushing myself to my limit and beyond and when I feel like I can't push anymore, I find the strength to push past what I feel. I can feel the air pressure change into an upward draft as I make my passes; I can feel my speed increase more and more and it's exhilarating. I know that maybe I should be afraid for my life but, right now the danger around me seems irrelevant. Everything is going to be okay. I can't explain it, but I know every-thing is going to be okay. I'm doing my best and I know I can outdo this sucker who was so arrogant as to think I would just surrender to his every whim.

As I go around and around, I see my past: how I started out in gymnastics wearing a leotard, swinging on loops and cartwheeling on balance beams. I see how my dad took me to boxing because I came home with too many black eyes and how I grasped the art so fast and so well that he put me in karate to make it challenging for me. I see how I met the PGs: Roy, Mark, and John and how we truly ventured out as friends on our second run. How that day was just about learning how to breathe so I wouldn't get winded too fast. I also see the third month when I did my first wall run and the exhil-aration I felt was like what I'm feeling now, but now more of it.

I can even see a few days ago when I started flying and how I documented the evidence today to show my family and to show myself that I wasn't crazy. I guess that could count as my present, but the last thing I see is different. You can call me crazy, but I think I can see a young woman who looks almost like Nurse May, but her hair is shorter. I see an island in the middle of the ocean that looks like a futuristic utopia and there are people there, but can do different things. What is this? Can this be the future or something?

As I ponder on these things, I hear a loud pop in my ear and I find the vapor is completely at my mercy. I think I've created the cycle that I need for my tornado or vacuum or whatever it is I'm doing. Right now, I'm sucking it up all the poison into the upper atmosphere where it is out of Belial's range of manipulation. I can see he's freaked out right now and most of the gas is gone. What he has left is just that needle and syringe in his hand with the green chemical he shot me with earlier. I know exactly what to do with it. After all the gas is sucked up so that there isn't enough to harm me with, I swoop down toward Belial and hit him with a well-aimed punch to his jaw. At the speed I'm going, he should have a bad headache.

I send him flying off the roof and the and the syringe goes flying out of his hand. I grab it and inject him with his own medicine. He lets out a scream and I catch him before he hits the ground. I sit him down and he seems unconscious. I walk away from him backward so that he doesn't pull a fast one on me like Tony did. He wakes up and tells me to wait so he can speak with me. I ignore it and continue to go to the place where the van is but he yells, "Stop! You are in more danger than you realize." I stop and listen to what he has to say because I can't take a statement like that lightly. If more of these people are going to attack me, I need to know how to defend against them.

"Listen to me Jason. The vile you injected me with was meant to aid in the mind-opening process."

I interrupt him angrily. "Is that what you call it?! Why would I open my mind to be like you?"

He continues, "Listen to me, young man. I am an agent of *dark* and I am sent to find others like us so that they could join us. Sometimes that requires an aided change of mind, but you injected me with it and right now I am using those chemicals in my body to cause severe respiratory damage."

I look at him like he's crazy and ask him why.

"Well, my dear boy, I have failed at my job and my employers don't take too kindly to failure. And rest assured, there are those with similar abilities like mine so it won't be a problem to find a replacement. I'm dead no matter what happens after this point. So I might as well tell you that I'm just like you. I found this power because I believed I could. But circumstances would have me to use my abilities for unfavorable characters. When you awoke this ability, you fell into a war and if there is *dark,* then you know there is *light* as well. There are others like us on each side of the chess board and each army is constantly recruiting members for their cause. They may have already paid you a visit and you just don't know it yet. But soon the *light* will make themselves known to you, just as they revealed themselves to me. And trust me, when they do, you must know that there can be no middle ground. In this war, you will either serve the *light* or *dark.* I once served *light,* but I am a man of logic and reason so I found my talents to be better suited for the *dark.* So young man, where will your talents be best suited, for I see a promising career in either?"

I ponder on what he says for a few moments and give him an answer. "I hate to burst your bubble, doc, but me and you are nothing alike. You chose to work for people who send you out like a mad dog to brainwash and kill people. You aren't a man of reason or logic; you are a man of chaos and death. I would never force this life on anybody and I don't care who you used to work for. They can come knocking on my door all they want. The answer is 'No.'

I'm nobody's pawn or soldier. And if they have a hard time taking no for an answer, then I will put them on the ground like you."

He smiles at me and says, "Very good young man. Very good."

He stops breathing and I rush to my family but the van that they were in is empty.

I rush into the air, panicking because the family that I just rescued is gone. I have no idea where to look. Was that last minute speech just a distraction to keep me away from them? I have absolutely no idea where to look. I then receive a phone call from my dad. I pick up with haste and hear a woman's voice on the phone: "Your family is safe at home, be there to greet them when they wake." She hangs up, but I have no idea who that was; it wasn't Nurse May's voice. This woman sounded younger. There's no time to wonder who this is, so I just rush home to help my family.

When I get home, I burst through the door and I find the biggest shock of my life. Our house is clean again and it's like no one ever trashed it. Man, I hope I'm not flipping out this late in the day because of all that poison. I rush upstairs to my brother's room and find him in bed fine. I check his vitals to make sure there is no labored breathing and he is just fine. I check on my sister Bella next and she is sleeping sloppily in her bed just like any other day. She is drooling so I know she is fine and she mumbles in her sleep about telling on me so I definitely know she's okay. The last I check are my parents and my dad doesn't even look as bad as he did when I saw him. My main concern is my mother lying next to him. She is in sweet sleep right now, but I'm going to wake them to tell them about all that happened. I hope they believe me when I tell them what happened.

Chapter 11

Keep Believing

I awake my mother and father to see how they are doing. My momma wakes first and my dad wakes behind her with groaning, probably feeling the effects of the scuffle he had with the goon who broke into our house. I can't imagine how he will feel when I tell him his friend was a sociopath who tried to kill us all, but he has to know.

I ask how they are doing and they reply in the oddest of ways.

My mother says, "JJ, what you doing here? I thought you were out for a run?"

I think to myself, *a run?* My dad awakes and sees the shape I'm in and asks me what happened. Before I answer him, I ask him, "Dad, do you remember calling anyone about me?"

He answers, "No."

I ask my mom if she was expecting anybody concerning me. She gives me a different response altogether. "Boy! No, now answer your father who put they hands on my baby. You just got back in school and you're already in another fight?!"

I calm my mother down and assure her that this didn't happen at school, but before I can tell her about all that's happened, my brother comes in and sees my condition. "Hey bro, did Tony do this to you?"

I'm looking at my family, wondering what is going on. They are acting like they don't know about the people who were here. Bella comes in starts instigating because of the bruises I have and I grow agitated and come out and say it.

"Dad, do you know who Doctor Belial is?"

He answers roughly "Yeah that is an old friend of mine, but I haven't heard or seen him for years. I was actually thinking of calling him later. Why did you happen to run into him? What? Did he do this to you?"

I want to say a big fat "*Yes*," but they don't seem to remember the man tried to kill us. It's like they all have amnesia or something. I hate to keep secrets, but I have a feeling trying to explain all of what happened would be harder than it sounds, and I don't have the patience for it. But I remember the documentary I made earlier and decide to show them tomorrow. For now, I say I had a rough workout down at the abandoned mill and I met Belial on my way home.

My mother scolds me for going to the old mill without anyone knowing and my dad tells me to be more careful and says he will talk to his old friend later. I hate to tell him that his friend virtually committed suicide because his employers would try to kill him. But I'm going to tell him about it all tomorrow. There will be no more secrets on my end. Everyone in my house will know what I can do starting early in the morning.

It was about ten o'clock when I got home, but nobody noticed, so I decided to deal with that in the morning as well. Today has been a long day and I just want to take a shower and put a lot of Icy Hot on my body. Everyone is asleep by the time I get out of the shower but at least it's quiet for the first time today. I decide to go my room to open the documentary file on my computer just for the sake of opening it. When I go into my room, I find the disc I hid with the note to my brother before I open the file I saved. Before I click the file to open it, I feel a swift sharp pain in my neck. The next thing I know I'm on the floor unable to move all over again! I have limited mobility and I feel like I'm losing consciousness.

I look over my shoulder and see a womanly figure emerge from the shadows. My first thought is, *Nurse May has come to pay me a visit but in a rude way.* As she comes closer, I see she is not Nurse May, but she looks an awful lot like her. As a matter of fact, she is the girl I saw in my vision when I was creating that vortex when I fought Belial. She looks at me and smirks, so I think she is going to kill me. I'm at her mercy. She walks over me and takes the disc from my hand and does something weird to my computer. She turns to me and says, "We have nullified the poison in your family's system but the process may have caused some memory loss. The little treatment I have just given you has should take care of any leftover poison that Belial may have hit you with. You shouldn't try to tell your family about the events of today just yet. We will show ourselves to you all in due time. Just be patient."

I'm steadily losing consciousness and just before I black out, I see her kneel down toward me and say the same words that May said to me but with her own flare. "Keep believing, little pilot."

If I didn't know any better, I'd say this was one of Mark's friends. He called me "little pilot" when he ended our friendship. Or has Nurse May and this mysterious girl been spying on me? Before I can ponder it anymore, I black out and I feel something press against my face, but I'm not sure what it is. I wake up several hours later and jump to my feet and wonder if it was a dream, but I can't find the DVD I just had. I check in the video camera and there is nothing in it! Maybe the file is still on my computer, but I check, and I see nothing! Man, somebody was in my room!

I open the window and blast out of my room window to the front yard. The force of my flight is so strong that the shockwave shakes every car and causes the alarms to go off. I'm so angry that someone else got the drop on me that I don't care who sees me in the air. As I look around to see where that woman could have gone, I hear my little brother call my name.

"JJ?"

I look back and see my brother stare at me with his jaw hanging low, speechless. Jackie is standing on the porch, looking at me suspended in the air. Now I do care about people seeing me and I don't even know if Jackie will keep this secret. This day just keeps getting better and better.

CPSIA information can be obtained
at www.ICGtesting.com
Printed in the USA
BVHW052122160123
656373BV00013B/1142